Joaquin Miller

Songs of the Sierras and Sunlands

Joaquin Miller

Songs of the Sierras and Sunlands

Joaquin Miller

Songs of the Sierras and Sunlands

ISBN/EAN: 9783743349414

Manufactured in Europe, USA, Canada, Australia, Japa

Cover: Foto ©Andreas Hilbeck / pixelio.de

Manufactured and distributed by brebook publishing software (www.brebook.com)

Yours.

Joaquin Miller

Songs of the Sierras

and Sunlands

(TWO VOLUMES IN ONE.)

By JOAQUIN MILLER,

AUTHOR OF "SONGS OF SUMMER LANDS," "IN CLASSIC
SHADES," ETC.

"The earth hath bubbles, as the water ha[s]
And these are of them."

PUBLISHERS.
W. B. CONKEY COMPANY,
CHICAGO.

CONTENTS.

SONGS OF THE SIERRAS.

ARIZONIAN.

" And I have said, and I say it ever,
   As the years go on and the world goes over,
'Twere better to be content and clever,
In the tending of cattle and the tossing of
      clover,
In the grazing of cattle and growing of grain,
Than a strong man striving for fame or gain;
Be even as kine in the red-tipp'd clover:
For they lie down and their rests are rests,
And the days are theirs, come sun, come rain,
To rest, rise up, and repose again;
While we wish and yearn, and pray in vain,
And hope to ride on the billows of bosoms,
' And hope to rest in the haven of breasts,
Till the heart is sicken'd and the fair hope
      dead—
Be even as clover with its crown of blossoms,
Even as blossoms ere the bloom is shed,

Kiss'd by the kine and the brown sweet bee—
For these have the sun, and moon, and air,
And never a bit of the burthen of care:
And with all of our caring what more have we?

"I would court content like a lover lonely,
I would woo her, win her, and wear her only.
I would never go over the white sea wall
For gold or for glory or for aught at all."

He said these things as he stood with the
     Squire
By the river's rim in the fields of clover,
While the stream flow'd on and the clouds flew
     over,
With the sun tangled in and the fringes afire.

So the squire lean'd with a kindly glory
To humor his guest, and to hear his story;
For his guest had gold, and he yet was clever,
And mild of manner; and, what was more, he,
In the morning's ramble had praised the kine,
The clover's reach and the meadows fine,
And so made the Squire his friend forever.

His brow was brown'd by the sun and
    weather,
And touch'd by the terrible hand of time;
His rich black beard had a fringe of rime,
As silk and silver inwove together.
There were hoops of gold all over his hands,
And across his breast, in chains and bands,
Broad and massive as belts of leather.

And the belts of gold were bright in the sun,
But brighter than gold his black eyes shone
From their sad face-setting so swarth and dun—
Brighter than beautiful Santan stone,
Brighter even than balls of fire,
As he said, hot-faced, in the face of the
    Squire:—

"The pines bow'd over, the stream bent un-
    der,
The cabin was cover'd with thatches of palm
Down in a canôn so deep, the wonder
Was what it could know in its clime but calm;
Down in a canôn so cleft asunder
By sabre-stroke in the young world's prime,
It look'd as if broken by bolts of thunder,

And burst asunder and rent and riven
By earthquakes driven that turbulent time
The red cross lifted red hands to heaven.

"And this in that land where the sun goes
    down,
And gold is gather'd by tide and by stream,
And maidens are brown as the cocoa brown,
And a life is a love and a love is a dream;
Where the winds come in from the far Ca-
    thay
With odor of spices and balm and bay,
And summer abideth with man alway,
Nor comes in a tour with the stately June,
And comes too late and returns too soon,

"She stood in the shadows as the sun went
    down,
Fretting her hair with her fingers brown,
As tall as the silk-tipp'd tassel'd corn—
Stood watching as I weighed the gold
We had wash'd that day where the river roll'd;
And her proud lip curl'd with a sun-clime
    scorn,

As she ask'd, ' Is she better or fairer than I?—
She, that blonde in the land beyond,
Where the sun is hid and the seas are high—
That you gather in gold as the years go by,
And hoard and hide it away for her
As a squirrel burrows the black pine-burr ?

   "Now the gold weigh'd well, but was lighter
      of weight
Than we two had taken for days of late,
So I was fretted, and brow a-frown,
I said, half-angered, with head held down—
'Well, yes, she is fairer; and I loved her first;
And shall love her last, come worst to the
      worst.'

   "Her lips grew livid, and her eyes afire
As I said this thing; and higher and higher
The hot words ran, when the booming thunder
Peal'd in the crags and the pine-tops under,
While up by the cliff in the murky skies
It look'd as the clouds had caught the fire—
The flash and fire of her wonderful eyes!

   "She turn'd from the door and down to the
      river,

And mirror'd her face in the whimsical tide;
Then threw back her hair as if throwing a
          quiver,
As an Indian throws it back far from his side
And free from his hands, swinging fast to the
          shoulder
When rushing to battle; and, turning, she
          sigh'd
And shook, and shiver'd as aspens shiver.

"Then a great green snake slid into the river,
Glistening green, and with eyes of fire;
Quick, double-handed she seized a boulder,
And cast it with all the fury of passion,
As with lifted head it went curving across,
Swift darting its tongue like a fierce desire,
Curving and curving, lifting higher and higher,
Bent and beautiful as a river moss;
Then, smitten, it turn'd, bent, broken and
          doubled
And lick'd, red-tongued, like a forked fire,
Till it made the very waters to shiver:
Then sank and the troubled waters bubbled
And so swept on in the old swift fashion.

"I lay in my hammock: the air was heavy

And hot and threat'ning; the very heaven
Was holding its breath; and bees in a bevy
Hid under my thatch; and birds were driven
In clouds to the rocks in a hurried whirr
As I peer'd down by the path for her.

"She stood like a bronze bent over the river,
The proud eyes fix'd, the passion unspoken.
Then the heavens broke like a great dyke
    broken;
And ere I fairly had time to give her
A shout of warning, a rushing of wind
And the rolling of clouds and a deafening din
And a darkness that had been black to the blind
Came down, as I shouted, 'Come in! Come in!
Come under the roof, come up from the river,
As up from the grave—come now,' or come
    never!'
The tassel'd tops of the pines were as weeds,
The red-woods rock'd like to lake-side reeds,
And the world seemed darken'd and drown'd
    forever,
While I crouched low; as a beast that bleeds.

"One time in the night as the black wind
    shifted,

And a flash of lightning stretch'd over the
    stream.
I seemed to see her with her brown hands
    lifted—
Only seem'd to see as one sees in a dream—
With her eyes wide wild and her pale lips
    press'd,
And the blood from her brow, and the flood to
    her breast;
When the flood caught her hair as flax in a
    wheel,
And wheeling and whirling her round like a
    reel;
Laugh'd loud her despair, then leapt like a steed,
Holding tight to her hair, folding fast to her
    heel,
Laughing fierce, leaping far as if spurr'd to its
    speed!

  "Now mind, I tell you all this did but seem—
Was seen as you see fearful scenes in a dream;
For what the devil could the lightning show
In a night like that, I should like to know!

  " And then I slept, and sleeping I dream'd

Of great green serpents with tongues of fire,
And of death by drowning, and of after death—
Of the day of judgment, wherein it seem'd
That she, the heathen, was bidden higher,
Higher than I; that I clung to her side,
And clinging struggled, and struggling cried,
And crying, wakened all weak of my breath.

" Long leaves of the sun lay over the floor,
And a chipmunk chirp'd at the open door.
But above on his crag the eagle scream'd,
Scream'd as he never had scream'd before.
I rush'd to the river: the flood had gone
Like a thief, with only his tracks upon
The weeds and grasses and warm wet sand;
And I ran after with reaching hand,
And call'd as I reach'd and reach'd as I ran,
And ran till I came to the canôn's van,
Where the waters lay in a bent lagoon,
Hook'd and crook'd like the horned moon.

"Lo! there in the surge where the waters
    met,
And the warm wave lifted, and the winds did
      fret

2

The wave till it foam'd with rage on the land,
She lay with the wave on the warm white sand;
Her rich hair trailed with the trailing weeds,
While her small brown hands lay prone or
     lifted
As the waves sang strophes in the broken reeds,
Or paused in pity, and in silence sifted
Sands of gold, as upon her grave.
And as sure as you see yon browsing kine,
And breathe the breath of your meadows fine,
When I went to my waist in the warm white
     wave
And stood all pale in the wave to my breast,
And reach'd my hands in her rest and unrest,
Her hands were lifted and reach'd to mine.

   " Now mind, I tell you, I cried, ' Come in!
Come into the house, come out from the hollow,
Come out of the storm, come up from the
     river!'
Cried, and call'd in that desolate din,
Though I did not rush out, and in plain words
     give her
A word warning of the flood to follow,
Word by word, and letter by letter:

But she knew it as well as I, and better;
For once in the desert of New Mexico
When we sought frantically far and wide
For the famous spot where the Apache shot
With bullets of gold their buffalo,
And she stood faithful to death at my side,
I threw me down in the hard hot sand
Utterly famish'd, and ready to die;
Then a speck arose in the red-hot sky—
A speck no larger than a lady's hand—
While she at my side bent tenderly over,
Shielding my face from the sun as a cover,
And wetting my face, as she watch'd by my
    side,
From a skin she had borne till the high noon-
    tide,
(I had emptied mine in the heat of the morning)
When the thunder mutter'd far over the plain
Like a monster bound or a beast in pain:
She sprang the instant, and gave the warning,
With her brown hand pointed to the burning
    skies,
For I was too weak unto death to rise.
But she knew the peril, and her iron will,
With a heart as true as the great North Star,

Did bear me up to the palm-tipp'd hill,
Where the fiercest beasts in a brotherhood,
Beasts that had fled from the plain and far,
In perfectest peace expectant stood,
With their heads held high, and their limbs
    a-quiver.
Then ere she barely had time to breathe
The boiling waters began to seethe
From hill to hill in a booming river,
Beating and breaking from hill to hill—
Even while yet the sun shot fire,
Without the shield of a cloud above—
Filling the canôn as you would fill
A wine-cup, drinking in swift desire,
With the brim new-kiss'd by the lips you love!

"So you see she knew—knew perfectly well,
As well as I could shout and tell,
That the mountain would send a flood to the
    plain,
Sweeping the gorge like a hurricane,
When the fire flash'd and the thunder fell.

"Therefore it is wrong, and I say therefore
Unfair, that a mystical, brown-wing'd moth

Or midnight bat should forevermore
Fan past my face with its wings of air,
And follow me up, down, everywhere,
Flit past, pursue me, or fly before,
Dimly limning in each fair place
The full fixed eyes and the sad, brown face,
So forty times worse than if it were wroth!

" I gather'd the gold I had hid in the earth,
Hid over the door and hid under the hearth:
Hoarded and hid, as the world went over,
For the love of a blonde by a sun-brown'd lover,
And I said to myself, as I set my face
To the East and afar from the desolate place,
'She has braided her tresses, and through her
    tears ·
Look'd away to the West for years, the years
That I have wrought where the sun tans brown;
She has waked by night, she has watch'd by day,
She has wept and wonder'd at my delay,
Alone and in tears, with her head held down,
Where the ships sail out and the seas swirl in,
Forgetting to knit and refusing to spin.

"She shall lift her head, she shall see her
    lover,

She shall hear his voice like a sea that rushes,
She shall hold his gold in her hands of snow,
And down on his breast she shall hide her
    blushes,
And never a care shall her true heart know,
While the clods are below, or the clouds are
    above her.'

"On the fringe of the night she stood with
    her pitcher
At the old town fountain: and oh! passing
    fair.
'I am riper now,' I said, 'but am richer,'
And I lifted my hand to my beard and hair;
'I am burnt by the sun, I am brown'd by the
    sea;
I am white of my beard, and am bald, may be;
Yet for all such things what can her heart
    care?'
Then she moved; and I said, 'How marvelous
    fair!'
She look'd to the West, with her arm arch'd
    over;
'Looking for me, her sun-brown'd lover,'
I said to myself, and my heart grew bold,

And I stepp'd me nearer to her presence there,
As approaching a friend; for 'twas here of old
Our troths were plighted and the tale was told.

" How young she was and how fair she was !
How tall as a palm, and how pearly fair,
As the night came down on her glorious hair !
Then the night grew deep and my eyes grew
          dim,
And a sad-faced figure began to swim
And float by my face, flit past, then pause,
With her hands held up and her head held
          down,
Yet face to face; and that face was brown !

" Now why did she come and confront me
          there,
With the flood to her face and the moist in her
          hair,
And a mystical stare in her marvelous eyes?
I had call'd to her twice, 'Come in! come in !
Come out of the storm to the calm within !'
Now, that is the reason I make complain
That for ever and ever her face should rise,
Facing face to face with her great sad eyes,

I said then to myself, and I say it again,
Gainsay it you, gainsay it who will,
I shall say it over and over still,
And will say it ever; I know it true,
That I did all that a man could do
(Some good men's doings are done in vain)
To save that passionate child of the sun,
With her love as deep as the doubled main,
And as strong and fierce as a troubled sea—
That beautiful bronze with its soul of fire,
Its tropical love and its kingly ire—
That child as fix'd as a pyramid,
As tall as a tula and pure as a nun—
And all there is of it, the all I did,
As often happens was done in vain.
So there is no bit of her blood on me.

" 'She is marvelous young and is wonderful
　　　fair,'
I said again, and my heart grew bold,
And beat and beat a charge for my feet.
'Time that defaces us, places, and replaces us,
And trenches our faces in furrows for tears,
Has traced here nothing in all these years.
'Tis the hair of gold that I vex'd of old,

The marvelous flowing flower of hair,
And the peaceful eyes in their sweet surprise
That I have kiss'd till the head swam round.
And the delicate curve of the dimpled chin,
And the pouting lips and the pearls within
Are the same, the same, but so young, so fair!'
My heart leapt out and back at a bound,
As a child that starts, then stops, then lingers.
'How wonderful young!' I lifted my fingers
And fell to counting the round years down
That I had dwelt where the sun tans brown.

"Four full hands, and a finger over!
'She does not know me, her truant lover,'
I said to myself, for her brow was a-frown
As I stepp'd still nearer, with my head held
    down,
All abash'd and in blushes my brown face
    over;
'She does not know me, her long lost lover,
For my beard's so long and my skin's so brown
That I well might pass myself for another.'
So I lifted my voice and I spake aloud:
"Annette, my darling! Annette Macleod!'
She started, she stopped, she turn'd, amazed,

She stood all wonder, her eyes wild-wide,
Then turn'd in terror down the dusk wayside,
And cried as she fled, 'The man he is crazed,
And he calls the maiden name of my mother!'

"Let the world turn over, and over, and over,
And toss and tumble like beasts in pain,
Crack, quake, and tremble, and turn full over
And die, and never rise up again;
Let her dash her peaks through the purple
        cover,
Let her plash her seas in the face of the sun—
I have no one to love me now, not one,
In a world as full as a world can hòld;
So I will get gold as I erst have done,
I will gather a coffin top-full of gold,
To take to the door of Death, to buy—
Buy what, when I double my hands and die?

    "Go down, go down to the fields of clover,
Go down with your kine to the pastures fine,
And give no thought, or care, or labor
For maid or man, good name or neighbor;
For I gave all as the years went over—
Gave all my youth, my years and labor,

And a heart as warm as the world is cold,
For a beautiful, bright, and delusive lie.
Gave youth, gave years, gave love for gold;
Giving and getting, yet what have I?

" The red ripe stars hang low overhead,
Let the good and the light of soul reach up.
Pluck gold as plucking a butter-cup:
But I am as lead, and my hands are red.

"So the sun climbs up, and on, and over,
And the days go out and the tides come in,
And the pale moon rubs on her purple cover
Till worn as thin and as bright as tin;
But the ways are dark and the days are dreary,
And the dreams of youth are but dust in age,
And the heart grows harden'd and the hands
        grow weary,
Holding them up for their heritage.

" For you promise so great and we gain so
        little;
For you promise so great of glory and gold,
And we gain so little that the hands grow cold,
And the strained heart-strings wear bare and
        brittle,

And for gold and glory we gain instead
A fond heart sicken'd and a fair hope dead.

"So I have said, and I say it over,
And can prove it over and over again,
That the four-footed beasts in the red-crown'd
     clover,
The pied and horned beasts on the plain
That lie down, rise up, and repose again,
And do never take care or toil or spin,
Nor buy, nor build, nor gather in gold,
Though the days go out and the tides come in,
Are better than we by a thousand fold;
For what is it all, in the words of fire,
But a vexing of soul and a vain desire?"

WITH WALKER IN NICARAGUA.

COME to my sunland! Come with me
To the land I love; where the sun and sea
Are wed for ever; where palm and pine
Are fill'd with singers; where tree and vine
Are voiced with prophets! O come, and you
Shall sing a song with the seas that swirl
And kiss their hands to that cold white girl,
To the maiden moon in her mantle of blue.

i.

HE was all man: let this be said
Above my brave dishonor'd dead.
I ask no more, this is not much,
Yet I disdain a colder touch
To memory as dear as his;
For he was true as God's north star,
And brave as Yuba's grizzlies are,
Yet gentle as a panther is,
Mouthing her young in her first fierce kiss.

A dash of sadness in his air,
Born, may be, of his over care,
And may be, born of a despair
In early love—I never knew;

I question'd not, as many do,
Of things as sacred as this is;
I only knew that he to me
Was all a father, friend, could be;
I sought to know no more than this
Of history of him or his.

A piercing eye, a princely air,
A presence like a chevalier,
Half angel and half Lucifer;
Sombrero black, with plume of snow
That swept his long silk locks below;
A red serape with bars of gold,
All heedless falling, fold on fold;
A sash of silk, where flashing swung
A sword as swift as serpent's tongue,
In sheath of silver chased in gold;
And Spanish spurs with bells of steel
That dash'd and dangled at the heel;
A face of blended pride and pain,
Of mingled pleading and disdain,
With shades of glory and of grief—
The famous filibuster chief
Stood by his tent amid the trees
That top the fierce Cordilleras,

With bent arm arch'd above his brow;—
Stood still—he stands, a picture, now—
Long gazing down the sunset seas.

II.

WHAT strange, strong, bearded men are these
He led toward the tropic seas!
Men sometimes of uncommon birth,
Men rich in histories untold,
Who boasted not, though more than bold,
Blown from the four parts of the earth.

Men mighty-thew'd as Samson was,
That had been kings in any cause,
A remnant of the races past;
Dark-brow'd as if in iron cast,
Broad-breasted as twin gates of brass,—
Men strangely brave and fiercely true,
Who dared the West when giants were,
Who err'd, yet bravely dared to err;
A remnant of that early few
Who held no crime or curse or vice
As dark as that of cowardice;

With blendings of the worst and best
Of faults and virtues that have blest
Or cursed or thrill'd the human breast.

They rode, a troop of bearded men,
Rode two and two out from the town,
And some were blonde and some were brown,
And all as brave as Sioux; but when
From San Bennetto south the line
That bound them in the laws of man
Was pass'd, and peace stood mute behind
And stream'd a banner to the wind
The world knew not, there was a sign
Of awe, of silence, rear and van.

Men thought who never thought before;
I heard the clang and clash of steel
From sword at hand or spur at heel
And iron feet, but nothing more.
Some thought of Texas, some of Maine,
But one of rugged Tennessee,—
And one of Avon thought, and one
Thought of an isle beneath the sun,
And one of Wabash, one of Spain,
And one turn'd sadly to the Spree.

Defeat meant something more than death;
The world was ready, keen to smite,
As stern and still beneath its ban
With iron will and bated breath,
Their hands against their fellow-man,
They rode—each man an Ishmaelite.
But when we struck the hills of pine,
These men dismounted, doff'd their cares,
Talk'd loud and laugh'd old love affairs,
And on the grass took meat and wine,
And never gave a thought again
To land or life that lay behind,
Or love, or care of any kind
Beyond the present cross or pain,

And I, a waif of stormy seas,
A child among such men as these,
Was blown along this savage surf
And rested with them on the turf,
And took delight below the trees.
I did not question, did not care
To know the right or wrong. I saw
That savage freedom had a spell,
And loved it more than I can tell,
And snapp'd my fingers at the law.

I bear my burden of the shame,—
I shun it not, and naught forget,
However much I may regret:
I claim some candor to my name,

And courage cannot change or die,—
Did they deserve to die? they died.
Let justice then be satisfied,
And as for me, why, what am I?

The standing side by side till death,
The dying for some wounded friend,
The faith that failed not to the end,
The strong endurance till the breath
And body took their ways apart,
I only know.   I keep my trust.
Their vices! earth has them by heart.
Their virtues! they are with their dust.

How wound we through the solid wood,
With all its broad boughs hung in green,
With lichen mosses trail'd between!
How waked the spotted beasts of prey,
Deep sleeping from the face of day,
And dashed them like a troubled flood
Down some defile and denser wood!

And snakes, long, lithe and beautiful
As green and graceful bough'd bamboo,
Did twist and twine them through and through
The boughs that hung red-fruited full.
One, monster-sized, above me hung,
Close eyed me with his bright pink eyes,
Then raised his folds, and sway'd and swung,
And lick'd like lightning his red tongue,
Then oped his wide mouth with surprise;
He writhed and curved and raised and low-
      er'd
His folds like liftings of the tide,
And sank so low I touch'd his side,
As I rode by, with my bright sword.

The trees shook hands high overhead,
And bow'd and intertwined across
The narrow way, while leaves and moss
And luscious fruit, gold-hued and red,
Through all the canopy of green,
Let not one sunshaft shoot between.

Birds hung and swung, green-robed and
      red,
Or droop'd in curved lines dreamily,

Rainbows reversed, from tree to tree,
Or sang low hanging overhead—
Sang low, as if they sang and slept,
Sang faint like some far waterfall,
And took no note of us at all,
Though nuts that in the way were spread
Did crush and crackle as we stept.

Wild lilies, tall as maidens are,
As sweet of breath, as pearly fair
As fair as faith, as pure as truth,
Fell thick before our every tread,
In fragrant sacrifice to ruth.
The ripen'd fruit a fragrance shed
And hung in hand-reach overhead,
In nest of blossoms on the shoot,
The bending shoot that bore the fruit.

How ran lithe monkeys through the
    leaves !
How rush'd they through, brown clad and
    blue,
Like shuttles hurried through and through
The threads a hasty weaver weaves!

How quick they cast us fruits of gold,

Then loosen'd hand and all foothold,
And hung limp, limber, as if dead,
Hung low and listless overhead;
And all the time with half-oped eyes
Bent full on us in mute surprise—
Look'd wisely, too, as wise hens do
That watch you with the head askew.

The long day through from blossom'd trees
There came the sweet song of sweet bees,
With chorus-tones of cockatoo
That slid his beak along the bough,
And walk'd and talk'd and hung and swung,
In crown of gold and coat of blue,
The wisest fool that ever sung,
Or had a crown, or held a tongue.

Oh! when we broke the somber wood
And pierced at last the sunny plain,
How wild and still with wonder stood
The proud mustangs with banner'd mane,
And necks that never knew a rein,
And nostrils lifted high, and blown,
Fierce breathing as a hurricane:
Yet by their leader held the while

In solid column, square, and file
And ranks more martial than our own !

Some one above the common kind,
Some one to look to, lean upon,
I think is much a woman's mind;
But it was mine, and I had drawn
A rein beside the chief while we
Rode through the forest leisurely;
When he grew kind and question'd me
Of kindred, home, and home affair,
Of how I came to wander there,
And had my father herds and land
And men in hundreds at command?
At which I silent shook my head,
Then, timid, met his eyes and said,
"Not so.   Where sunny-foot hills run
Down to the North Pacific sea,
And Willamette meets the sun
In many angles, patiently
My father tends his flocks of snow,
And turns alone the mellow sod
And sows some fields not over broad,
And mourns my long delay in vain,
Nor bids one serve-man come or go;

While mother from her wheel or churn,
And may be from the milking shed,
There lifts an humble, weary head
To watch and wish her boy's return
Across the camas' blossom'd plain."

He held his bent head very low,
A sudden sadness in his air;
Then turn'd and touch'd my yellow hair
And took the long locks in his hand,
Toy'd with them, smiled, and let them go,
Then thrumm'd about his saddle bow
As thought ran swift across his face;
Then turning sudden from his place,
He gave some short and quick command.
They brought the best steed of the band,
They swung a bright sword at my side,
He bade me mount and by him ride,
And from that hour to the end
I never felt the need of friend.

Far in the wildest quinine wood
We found a city old—so old,
Its very walls were turn'd to mould,
And stately trees upon them stood.

No history has mention'd it,
No map has given it a place; .
The last dim trace of tribe and race—
The world's forgetfulness is fit.

It held one structure grand and moss'd,
Mighty as any castle sung,
And old when oldest Ind was young,
With threshold Christian never cross'd;
A temple builded to the sun,
Along whose sombre altar-stone
Brown bleeding virgins had been strown
Like leaves, when leaves are crisp and dun,
In ages ere the Sphinx was born,
Or Babylon had birth or morn.
My chief led up the marble step—
He ever led, broad blade in hand—
When down the stones, with double hand
Clutched to his sword, a Sun priest leapt,
Hot bent to barter life for life.
The chieftain drove his bowie knife,
Full through his thick and broad breast-bone,
And broke the point against the stone,
The dark stone of the temple wall.
I saw him loose his hold and fall

Full length with head hung down the step;
I saw run down a ruddy flood
Of awful, pulsing human blood.
Then from the crowd a woman crept
And kiss'd the gory hands and face,
And smote herself.   Then one by one
The dark crowd crept and did the same,
Then bore the dead man from the place.
Down darken'd aisles the brown priests came,
So picture-like, with sandall'd feet
And long, grey, dismal, grass-wove gowns,
So like the pictures of old time,
And stood all still and dark of frowns,
At blood upon the stone and street.

So we laid ready hand to sword
And boldly spoke some bitter word;
But they were stubborn still, and stood
Fierce frowning as a winter wood,
And mutt'ring something of the crime
Of blood upon a temple stone,
As if the first that it had known.

We turn'd toward the massive door
With clash of steel at heel, and with

Some swords all red and ready drawn.
I traced the sharp edge of my sword
Along the marble wall and floor
For crack or crevice; there was none.
From one vast mount of marble stone
The mighty temple had been cored
By nut-brown children of the sun,
When stars were newly bright and blithe
Of song along the rim of dawn,
A mighty marble monolith!

    *   *   *   *   *

III.

    *   *   *   *   *

THROUGH marches through the mazy wood,
And may be through too much of blood,
At last we came down to the seas.
A city stood, white wall'd, and brown
With age, in nest of orange trees;
And this we won and many a town
And rancho reaching up and down,
Then rested in the red-hot days
Beneath the blossom'd orange trees,

Made drowsy with the drum of bees,
And drank in peace the south-sea breeze,
Made sweet with sweeping boughs of bays.

Well! there were maidens, shy at first,
And then, ere long, not over shy,
Yet pure of soul and proudly chare.
No love on earth has such an eye!
No land there is, is bless'd or curs'd
With such a limb or grace of face,
Or gracious form, or genial air!
In all the bleak North-land not one
Hath been so warm of soul to me
As coldest soul by that warm sea,
Beneath the bright hot centred sun.

No lands where northern ices are
Approach, or ever dare compare
With warm loves born beneath the sun,
The one the cold white steady star,
The lifted shifting sun the one.
I grant you fond, I grant you fair,
I grant you honor, trust and truth,
And years as beautiful as youth,
And many years beneath the sun,

And faith as fix'd as any star;
But all the North-land hath not one
So warm of soul as sun-maids are.

I was but in my boyhood then,
I count my fingers over, so,
And find it years and years ago,
And I am scarcely yet of men,
But I was tall and lithe and fair,
With rippled tide of yellow hair,
And prone to mellowness of heart;
While she was tawny-red like wine,
With black hair boundless as the night,
As for the rest I knew my part,
At least was apt, and willing quite
To learn, to listen, and incline
To teacher warm and wise as mine.

O bright, bronzed maidens of the Sun!
So fairer far to look upon
Than curtains of the Solomon,
Or Kedar's tents, or any one,
Or any thing beneath the sun!
What follow'd then? What has been done,
And said, and writ, and read, and sung?

What will be writ and read again,
While love is life, and life remain?—
While maids will heed, and men have
      tongue?

  What follow'd then? But let that pass.
I hold one picture in my heart,
Hung curtain'd, and not any part
Of all its dark tint ever has
Been look'd upon by any one
Beneath the broad all-seeing sun.

  Love well who will, love wise who can,
But love, be loved, for God is love;
Love pure, like cherubim above;
Love maids, and hate not any man.
Sit as sat we by orange tree,
Beneath the broad bough and grape-vine
Top-tangled in the tropic shine,
Close face to face, close to the sea,
And full of the red-centred sun,
With grand sea-songs upon the soul,
Roll'd melody on melody,
Like echoes of deep organ's roll,
And love, nor question any one.

If God is love, is love not God?
As high priests say, let prophets sing,
Without reproach or reckoning;
This much I say, knees knit to sod,
And low voice lifted, questioning.

Let hearts be pure and strong and true,
Let lips be luscious and blood-red,
Let earth in gold be garmented
And tented in her tent of blue.
Let goodly rivers glide between
Their leaning willow walls of green,
Let all things be fill'd of the sun,
And full of warm winds of the sea,
And I beneath my vine and tree
Take rest, nor war with any one;
Then I will thank God with full cause,
Say this is well, is as it was.

Let lips be red, for God has said
Love is like one gold-garmented,
And made them so for such a time.
Therefore let lips be red, therefore
Let love be ripe in ruddy prime,
Let hope beat high, let hearts be true,

And you be wise thereat, and you
Drink deep, and ask not any more.

   Let red lips lift, proud curl'd to kiss,
And round limbs lean and raise and reach
In love too passionate for speech,
   Too full of blessedness and bliss
For anything but this and this;
Let luscious lips lean hot to kiss
And swoon in love, while all the air
Is redolent with balm of trees,
And mellow with the song of bees,
While birds sit singing everywhere—
And you will have not any more
Than I in boyhood, by that shore
Of olives, had in years of yore.

   Let the unclean think things unclean;
I swear tip-toed, with lifted hands,
That we were pure as sea-wash'd sands,
That not one coarse thought came between;
Believe or disbelieve who will,
Unto the pure all things are pure;
As for the rest, I can endure
Alike their good will or their ill.

Aye! she was rich in blood and gold—
More rich in love, grown over-bold
From its own consciousness of strength.
How warm! Oh, not for any cause
Could I declare how warm she was,
In her brown beauty and hair's length.
We loved in the sufficient sun,
We lived in elements of fire,
For love is fire and fierce desire;
Yet lived as pure as priest and nun.

We lay slow rocking in the bay
In birch canoe beneath the crags
Thick-topp'd with palm, like sweeping flags
Between us and the burning day.
The alligator's head lay low
Or lifted from' his rich rank fern,
And watch'd us and the tide by turn,
As we slow cradled to and fro.

And slow we cradled on till night,
And told the old tale, overtold,
As misers in recounting gold
Each time to take a new delight.
With her pure passion-given grace
She drew her warm self close to me;

And her two brown hands on my knee,
And her two black eyes in my face,
She then grew sad and guess'd at ill,
And in the future seem'd to see
With woman's ken of prophecy;
Yet proffer'd her devotion still.
And plaintive so she gave a sign,
A token cut of virgin gold,
That all her tribe should ever hold
Its wearer as some one divine,
Nor touch him with a hostile hand.
And I in turn gave her a blade,
A dagger, worn as well by maid
As man, in that half lawless land.
It had a massive silver hilt,
It had a keen and cunning blade,
A gift by chief and comrades made
For reckless blood at Rivas split.
"Show this," said I, "too well 'tis known,
And worth a hundred lifted spears,
Should ill beset your sunny years;
There is not one in Walker's band,
But at the sight of this alone,
Will reach a brave and ready hand,
And make your right or wrong his own."

4

IV.

Love while 'tis day; night cometh soon,
Wherein no man or maiden may;
Love in the strong young prime of day;
Drink drunk with love in ripe red noon,
Red noon of love and life and sun;
Walk in love's light as in sunshine,
Drink in that sun as drinking wine,
Drink swift, nor question any one;
For loves change sure as man or moon,
And wane like warm full days of June.

Oh Love, so fair of promises,
Bend here thy brow, blow here thy kiss,
Bend here thy bow above the storm
But once, if only this once more.
Comes there no patient Christ to save,
Touch and re-animate thy form
Long three days dead and in the grave?
Spread here thy silken net of jet;
Since man is false, since maids forget,
Since man must fall for some sharp sin,
Be thou the pit that I fall in;

I seek no safer fall than this.
Since man must die for some dark sin,
Blind leading blind, let come to this,
And my death crime be one deep kiss.

V.

ILL comes disguised in many forms:
Fair winds are but a prophecy
Of foulest winds full soon to be—
The brighter these, the blacker they;
The clearest night has darkest day,
And brightest days bring blackest storms.
There came reverses to our arms;
I saw the signal-light's alarms
At night red-crescenting the bay.
The foe pour'd down a flood next day
As strong as tides when tides are high,
And drove us bleeding to the sea,
In such wild haste of flight that we
Had hardly time to arm and fly.

  Blown from the shore, borne far a-sea,
I lifted my two hands on high

With wild soul plashing to the sky,
And cried, "O more than crowns to me,
Farewell at last to love and thee!"
I walk'd the deck, I kiss'd my hand
Back to the far and fading shore,
And bent a knee as to implore,
Until the last dark head of land
Slid down behind the dimpled sea.
At last I sank in troubled sleep,
A very child, rock'd by the deep,
Sad questioning the fate of her
Before the savage conqueror.

The loss of comrades, power, place,
A city wall'd, cool shaded ways,
Cost me no care at all; somehow
I only saw her sad brown face,
And—I was younger then than now.

Red flashed the sun across the deck,
Slow flapp'd the idle sails, and slow
The black ship cradled to and fro.
Afar my city lay, a speck
Of white against a line of blue;
Around, half lounging on the deck,

Some comrades chatted two by two.
I held a new-fill'd glass of wine,
And with the mate talk'd as in play
Of fierce events of yesterday,
To coax his light life into mine.

He jerked the wheel, as slow he said,
Low laughing with averted head,
And so, half sad: "You bet they'll fight;
They follow'd in canim, canoe,
A perfect fleet, that on the blue
Lay dancing till the mid of night.
Would you believe! one little cuss"—
(He turn'd his stout head slow sidewise,
And 'neath his hat-rim took the skies)—
"In petticoats did follow us
The livelong night, and at the dawn
Her boat lay rocking in the lee,
Scarce one short pistol-shot from me."
This said the mate, half mournfully,
Then peck'd at us; for he had drawn,
By bright light heart and homely wit,
A knot of us around the wheel,
Which he stood whirling like a reel,
For the still ship reck'd not of it.

"And where's she now?" one careless said,
With eyes slow lifting to the brine,
Swift swept the instant far by mine;
The bronzed mate listed, shook his head,
Spirted a stream of amber wide
Across and over the ship side,
Jerk'd at the wheel, and slow replied

"She had a dagger in her hand,
She rose, she raised it, tried to stand,
But fell, and so upset herself;
Yet still the poor brown savage elf,
Each time the long light wave would toss
And lift her form from out the sea,
Would shake a strange bright blade at me,
With rich hilt chased a cunning cross.
At last she sank, but still the same
She shook her dagger in the air,
As if to still defy and dare,
And sinking seem'd to call your name."

I let my wine glass crashing fall,
I rush'd across the deck, and all
The sea I swept and swept again,
With lifted hand, with eye and glass,

But all was idle and in vain.
I saw a red-bill'd sea-gull pass,
A petrel sweeping round and round,
I heard the far white sea-surf sound,
But no sign could I hear or see
Of one so more than seas to me.

I cursed the ship, the shore, the sea,
The brave brown mate, the bearded men;
I had a fever then, and then
Ship, shore and sea were one to me;
And weeks we on the dead waves lay,
And I more truly dead than they.
At last some rested on an isle;
The few strong-breasted, with a smile,
Returning to the hostile shore,
Scarce counting of the pain or cost,
Scarce recking if they won or lost;
They sought but action, ask'd no more;
They counted life but as a game,
With full per cent. against them, and
Staked all upon a single hand,
And lost or won, content the same.

I never saw my chief again,
I never sought again the shore,

Or saw my white-wall'd city more.
I could not bear the more than pain
At sight of blossom'd orange trees
Or blended song of birds and bees,
The sweeping shadows of the palm
Or spicy breath of bay and balm.
And, striving to forget the while,
I wander'd through the dreary isle,
Here black with juniper, and there
Made white with goats in shaggy coats,
The only things that anywhere
We found with life in all the land,
Save birds that ran long-bill'd and brown,
Long legg'd and still as shadows are,
Like dancing shadows up and down
The sea-rim on the swelt'ring sand.

The warm sea laid his dimpled face,
With all his white locks smoothed in place,
As if asleep against the land;
Great turtles slept upon his breast,
As thick as eggs in any nest;
I could have touch'd them with my hand.

VI.

I WOULD some things were dead and hid,

Well dead and buried deep as hell,
With recollection dead as well,
And resurrection God-forbid.
They irk me with their weary spell
Of fascination, eye to eye,
And hot mesmeric serpent hiss,
Through all the dull eternal days.
Let them turn by, go on their ways,
Let them depart or let me die;
For life is but a beggar's lie,
And as for death, I grin at it;
I do not care one whiff or whit
Whether it be or that or this.

I give my hand; the world is wide;
Then farewell memories of yore,
Between us let strife be no more;
Turn as you choose to either side;
Say, Fare-you-well, shake hands and say—
Speak loud, and say with stately grace,
Hand clutching hand, face bent to face—
Farewell forever and a day.

O passion-toss'd and bleeding past,
Part now, part well, part wide apart,

As ever ships on ocean slid
Down, down the sea, hull, sail and mast;
And in the album of my heart
Let hide the pictures of your face,
With other pictures in their place,
Slid over like a coffin's lid.

VII.

THE days and grass grow long together;
They now fell short and crisp again,
And all the fair face of the main
Grew dark and wrinkled as the weather.
Through all the summer sun's decline
Fell news of triumphs and defeats,
Of hard advances, hot retreats—
Then days and days and not a line.

At last one night they came. I knew
Ere yet the boat had touch'd the land
That all was lost; they were so few
I near could count them on one hand;
But he, the leader, led no more.
The proud chief still disdain'd to fly,

But like one wreck'd, clung to the shore,
And struggled on, and struggling fell
From power to a prison-cell,
And only left that cell to die.

My recollection, like a ghost,
Goes from this sea to that sea-side,
Goes and returns as turns the tide,
Then turns again unto the coast.
I know not which I mourn the most,
My chief or my unwedded wife.
The one was as the lordly sun,
To joy in, bask in, and admire;
The peaceful moon was as the one,
To love, to look to, and desire;
And both a part of my young life.

VIII.

YEARS after, shelter'd from the sun
Beneath a Sacramento bay,
A black Muchacho by me lay
Along the long grass crisp and dun,
His brown mule browsing by his side.
And told with all a Peon's pride

How he once fought;how long and well,
Broad breast to breast, red hand to hand,
Against a foe for his fair land,
And how the fierce invader fell;
And, artless, told me how he died.

He walked out from the prison-wall
Dress'd like some prince for a parade,
And made no note of man or maid,
But gazed out calmly over all.
He look'd far off, half paused, and then
Above the mottled sea of men
He kiss'd his thin hand to the sun;
Then smiled so proudly none had known
But he was stepping to a throne,
Yet took no note of any one.

A nude brown beggar Peon child,
Encouraged as the captive smiled,
Look'd up, half scared, half pitying;
He stopp'd, he caught it from the sands,
Put bright coins in its two brown hands,
Then strode on like another king.

Two deep, a musket's length, they stood

A-front, in sandals, nude, and dun
As death and darkness wove in one,
Their thick lips thirsting for his blood.
He took their black hands one by one,
And, smiling with a patient grace,
Forgave them all and took his place.
He bared his broad brow to the sun,
Gave one long, last look to the sky,
The white wing'd clouds that hurried by,
The olive hills in orange hue;
A last list to the cockatoo
That hung by beak from cocoa-bough
Hard by, and hung and sung as though
He never was to sing again,
Hung all red-crown'd and robed in green,
With belts of gold and blue between.—

A bow, a touch of heart, a pall
Of purple smoke, a crash, a thud,
A warrior's raiment rent, and blood,
A face in dust and—that was all.

Success had made him more than king;
Defeat made him the vilest thing
In name, contempt or hate can bring:

So much the leaded dice of war
Do make or mar of character.

Speak ill who will of him, he died
In all disgrace; say of the dead
His heart was black, his hands were red—
Say this much, and be satisfied;
Gloat over it all undenied.
I simply say he was my friend
When strong of hand and fair of fame:
Dead and disgraced, I stand the same
To him, and so shall to the end.

I lay this crude wreath on his dust,
Inwove with sad, sweet memories
Recall'd here by these colder seas.
I leave the wild bird with his trust,
To sing and say him nothing wrong;
I wake no rivalry of song.

He lies low in the levell'd sand,
Unshelter'd from the tropic sun,
And now of all he knew not one
Will speak him fair in that far land.
Perhaps 'twas this that made me seek,

Disguised, his grave one winter-tide;
A weakness for the weaker side,
A siding with the helpless weak.

A palm not far held out a hand,
Hard by a long green bamboo swung,
And bent like some great bow unstrung,
And quiver'd like a willow wand;
Beneath a broad banana's leaf,
Perch'd on its fruits that crooked hang,
A bird in rainbow splendor sang
A low, sad song of temper'd grief.

No sod, no sign, no cross nor stone
But at his side a cactus green
Upheld its lances long and keen;
It stood in sacred sands alone,
Flat-palm'd and fierce with lifted spears;
One bloom of crimson crown'd its head,
A drop of blood, so bright, so red,
Yet redolent as roses' tears.

In my left hand I held a shell,
All rosy lipp'd and pearly red;
I laid it by his lowly bed,

For he did love so passing well
The grand songs of the solemn sea.
O shell! sing well, wild, with a will,
When storms blow loud and birds be still,
The wildest sea-song known to thee!

I said some things, with folded hands,
Soft whisper'd in the dim sea-sound,
And eyes held humbly to the ground,
And frail knees sunken in the sands.
He had done more than this for me,
And yet I could not well do more:
I turn'd me down the olive shore,
And set a sad face to the sea.

ROOM! Room to turn round in, to breathe and be free,
    To grow to be giant, to sail as at sea
With the speed of the wind on a steed with his mane
To the wind, without pathway or route or a rein.
Room! Room to be free where the white-border'd sea
Blows a kiss to a brother as boundless as he.
Where the buffalo come like a cloud on the plain,
Pouring on like the tide of a storm-driven main,
And the lodge of the hunter to friend or to foe
Offers rest; and unquestion'd you come or you go.
My plains of America! Seas of wild lands!
From a land in the seas in a raiment of foam,
That has reached to a stranger the welcome of home,
I turn to you, lean to you, lift you my hands.
LONDON, 1871.

RUN? Now you bet you; I rather guess so!
    But he's blind as a badger.   Whoa, Pache,
        boy, whoa.
No, you wouldn't believe it to look at his eyes,
But he's blind, badger blind, and it happen'd
        this wise:

"We lay   in the grasses and the sunburnt
        clover

That spread on the ground like a great brown
     cover
Northward and southward, and west and away
To the Brazos, to where our lodges lay,
One broad and unbroken level of brown.
We were waiting the curtains of night to come
     down
To cover us over and conceal our flight
With my brown bride, won from an Indian town
That lay in the rear the full ride of a night.

"We lounged in the grasses—her eyes were in
     mine,
And her hands on my knee, and her hair was
     as wine
In its wealth and its flood, pouring on and all
     over
Her bosom wine-red, and press'd never by one.
Her touch was as warm as the tinge of the
     clover
Burn't brown as it reach'd to the kiss of the sun.
Her words they were low as the lute-throated
     dove,
And as laden with love as the heart when it
     beats

In its hot, eager answer to earliest love,
Or the bee hurried home by its burthen of
    sweets.

We lay low in the grass on the broad
    plain levels,
Old Revels and I, and my stolen brown bride;
"Forty full miles if a foot to ride!
Forty full miles if a foot, and the devils
Of red Comanches are hot on the track
When once they strike it. Let the sun go down
Soon, very soon," muttered bearded old Revels
As he peer'd at the sun, lying low on his back,
Holding fast to his lasso. Then he jerk'd at
    his steed
And he sprang to his feet, and glanced swiftly
    around,
And then dropp'd, as if shot, with an ear to
    the ground;
Then again to his feet, and to me, to my bride,
While his eyes were like fire, his face like a
    shroud,
His form like a king, and his beard like a cloud,
And his voice loud and shrill, as if blown from
    a reed,—

'Pull, pull in your lassoes, and bridle to steed,
And speed you if ever for life you would
        speed.
Yea, ride for your lives, for your lives you must
        ride !
For the plain is aflame, the prairie on fire,
And feet of wild horses hard flying before
I hear like a sea breaking high on the shore,
While the buffalo come like a surge of the sea,
Driven far by the flame, driving fast on us
    ·   three
As a hurricane comes, crushing palms in his
        ire.'

"We drew in the lassoes, seized saddle and
        rein,
Threw them on, cinched them on, cinched
        them over again,
And again drew the girth; threw robes in a
        breath.
And bared to the skin, sprang all haste to the
        horse—
Sprang bare as when born, as when new from ·
        the hand
Of God—without speech or one word of com-
        mand.

Turn'd head to the Brazos in red race with
    death,

Turn'd head to the Brazos with breath in the
    hair;

Blowing hot from a king leaving death in his
    course,

Turn'd head to the Brazos with a sound in the
    air

Like the surge of a sea, and a flash in the eye,

Of a red wall of flame reaching up to the sky.

Stretching fierce in pursuit of a black rolling
    sea

Rushing fast upon us, as the wind sweeping
    free

And afar from the desert blew hollow and
    hoarse.

"Not a word, not a wail from a lip was let
    fall,

Not a kiss from my bride, not a look nor low
    call

Of love-note or courage; but on o'er the plain

So steady, so still, lean'd we low to the mane,

With the heel to the flank and the hand to the
    rein.

Rode we on, rode we three, rode we nose and
    reach'd nose,
Reaching long, breathing loud, as a creviced
    wind blows:
We broke not a whisper, we breathed not a
    prayer,
There was work to be done, there was death in
    the air,
And the chance was as one to a thousand
    for all.

"Grey nose to grey nose, and each steady
    mustang
Stretch'd neck and stretch'd nerve till the arid
    earth rang,
And the foam from the flank and the croup
    and the neck
Flew around like the spray on a storm-driven
    deck.
Twenty miles!....thirty miles!....a dim dis-
    tant speck....
Then a long reaching line, and the Brazos in
    sight!
And I rose in my seat with a shout of delight.
I stood in my stirrup and look'd to my right—

But Revels was gone; I glanced by my shoulder
And saw his horse stagger; I saw his head
    drooping
Hard down on his breast, and his naked breast
    stooping
Low down to the mane, as so swifter and bolder
Ran reaching out for us the red-footed fire.
To right and to left the black buffalo came,
A terrible surf to that red sea of flame.
He rode neck to neck with a buffalo bull,
That made the earth shake where he came in
    his course.
'Twas a monarch of millions, with shaggy mane
    full
Of smoke and of dust, and it shook with desire
Of battle, with rage and with bellowings hoarse.
His keen, crooked horns, through the storm of
    his mane,
Like black lances lifted and lifted again;
And I looked but this once, for the fire licked
    through,
And Revels was gone, as we rode two and two.

" I look'd to my left then—and nose, neck,
    and shoulder

Sank slowly, sank surely, till back to my thighs,
And up through the black blowing veil of her
       hair
Did beam full in mine her two marvelous eyes,
With a longing and love yet a look of despair
And of pity for me, as she felt the smoke fold
       her,
And flames reaching far for her glorious hair.
Her sinking steed falter'd, his eager ears fell
To and fro and unsteady, and all the neck's
       swell
Did subside and recede, and he fell and was
       gone
As I reach'd through the flame and I bore her
       still on.

"Then the rushing of fire around us and under,
And the howling of beasts and a sound as of
       thunder—
Beasts burning and blind and forced onward
       and over,
As the passionate flame reach'd round them,
       and wove her
Red hands in their hair, and kiss'd hot till they
       died—

Till they died with a wild and a desolate moan,
As a sea heart-broken on the hard brown stone—
And into the Brazos I rode all alone—
All alone, with my love on a horse long-limb'd,
And blinded and bare and burnt to the skin.
Then just as the terrible sea came in
And tumbled its thousands hot into the tide,
Till the tide block'd up and the swift stream
      brimm'd
With my bride on my breast we struck the
      far side.

Yes, there sits my bride in the shade of her
      palm;
Ay, still we are lovers, if that's aught to you..
She's a tawny, wild woman, but as true, sir, as
      true
As yon sun in heaven. And I—I am what I
      am."

THE LAST TASCHASTAS.

THE hills were brown, the heavens were blue,
A woodpecker pounded a pine-top shell,
While a partridge whistled the whole day through
For a rabbit to dance in the chapparal,
And a grey grouse drumm'd, "All's well, all's well."

I.

WRINKLED and brown as a bag of leather,
A squaw sits moaning long and low.
Yesterday she was a wife and mother,
To-day she is rocking her to and fro,
A childless widow, in weeds and woe.

An Indian sits in a rocky cavern
Whetting a flint in an arrow head;
His children are moving as still as shadows,
His squaw is moulding some balls of lead,
With round face painted all battle-red.
An Indian sits in a black-jack jungle,
Where a grizzly bear has rear'd her young,
Whetting a flint on a granite boulder.
His quiver is over his brown back hung—
His face is streak'd and his bow is strung

An Indian hangs from a cliff of granite,
Like an eagle's nest built in the air,
Looking away to the east, and watching
The smoke of the cabins curling there,
And eagle's feathers are in his hair.

In belt of wampum, in battle fashion,
An Indian watches with wild desire.
He is red with paint, he is black with passion;
And grand as a god in his savage ire,
He leans and listens till stars are a-fire.

All sombre and sullen and sad, a chieftain
Now looks from the mountain far into the sea.
Just before him beat in the white billows,
Just behind him the toppled tall tree
And chopping white woodmen, knee buckled
    to knee.

II.

ALL together, all in council,
In a canôn wall'd so high
That no thing could ever reach them

Save some stars dropp'd from the sky,
And the brown bats sweeping by:

Tawny chieftains thin and wiry,
Wise as brief, and brief as bold;
Chieftains young and fierce and fiery,
Chieftains stately tall, that told
Their counsellings like kings of old.

Flamed the council-fire brighter,
Flash'd black eyes like diamond beads,
When a woman told her sorrows,
While a warrior told his deeds,
And a widow tore her weeds.

Then was lit the pipe of council
That their fathers smoked of old,
With its stem of manzinnetta,
And its bowl of quartz and gold,
And traditions manifold.

Lo! from lip to lip in silence
Burn'd it round the circle red,
Like an evil star slow passing
(Sign of battles and blood shed)

Round the heavens overhead.
Then the silence deep was broken
By the thunder rolling far,
As gods muttering in anger,
Or the bloody battle-car
Of a Christian king at war.

"'Tis the spirits of my Fathers
Mutt'ring vengeance in the skies;
And the flashing of the lightning
Is the anger of their eyes,
Bidding us in battle rise,"

Cried the war-chief, now up-rising,
Naked all above the waist,
While a belt of shells and silver
Held his tamoos to its place,
And the war-paint streak'd his face.

Women melted from the council,
Boys crept backward out of sight,
Till alone a wall of warriors
In their paint and battle-plight
Sat reflecting back the light.

"O my Fathers in the storm-cloud!"
(Red arms tossing to the skies,
  While the massive walls of granite
  Seem'd to shrink to half their size,
  And to mutter strange replies)—

"Soon we come, O angry Fathers,
  Down the darkness you have cross'd:
  Speak for hunting-grounds there for us;
  Those you left us we have lost—
  Gone like blossoms in a frost:

"Warriors!" (and his arms fell folded
  On his tawny swelling breast,
  While his voice, now low and plaintive
  As the waves in their unrest,
  Touching tenderness confess'd),

"Where is Wrotto, wise of counsel,
  Yesterday here in his place?
  A brave lies dead down in the valley,
  Last brave of his line and race,
  And a Ghost sits on his face.

"Where his boy the tender-hearted,
  With his mother yestermorn?

Lo! a wigwam door is darkèn'd,
And a mother mourns forlorn,
With her long locks toss'd and torn.

"Lo! our daughters have been gather'd
From among us by the foe,
Like the lilies they once gather'd
In the spring-time all aglow
From the banks of living snow

"Through the land where we for ages
Laid the bravest, dearest dead,
Grinds the savage white-man's ploughshare
Grinding sires' bones for bread—
We shall give them blood instead.

" I saw white skulls in a furrow,
And around the cursed ploughshare
Clung the flesh of my own children.
And my mother's tangled hair
Trailed along the furrow there.

" Warriors! braves! I cry for vengeance !
And the dim ghosts of the dead
Unavenged do wail and shiver

In the storm cloud overhead,
And shoot arrows battle-red."
Then he ceased, and sat among them,
With his long locks backward strown;
They as mute as men of marble,
He a king upon the throne,
And as still as polished stone.

Then uprose the war-chief's daughter,
Taller than the tassell'd corn,
Sweeter than the kiss of morning,
Sad as some sweet star of morn,
Half defiant, half forlorn.

Robed in skins of stripéd panther
Lifting loosely to the air,
With a face a shade of sorrow
And black eyes that said, Beware!
Nestled in a storm of hair;

With her stripéd robes around her,
Fasten'd by an eagle's beak,
Stood she by the stately chieftain,
Proud and pure as Shasta's peak,
As she ventured thus to speak:

" Must the tomahawk of battle
Be unburied where it lies,
O, last war-chief of Taschastas?
Must the smoke of battle rise
Like a storm cloud in the skies?

"True, some wretch has laid a brother
With his swift feet to the sun,
But because one bough is broken,
Must the broad oak be undone?
All the red-wood fell'd as one?

"True, the braves have faded, wasted
Like ripe blossoms in the rain,
But when we have spent the arrows,
Do we twang the string in vain,
And then snap the bow in twain?"

Like a vessel in a tempest
Shook the warrior, wild and grim,
As he gazed out in the midnight,
As to things that beckon'd him,
And his eyes were moist and dim.

Then he turn'd, and to his bosom

6

Battle-scarr'd, and strong as brass,
Tenderly the warrior press'd her
As if she were made of glass,
Murmuring, "Alas! alas!

"Loua Ellah! Spotted Lily!
Streaks of blood shall be the sign,
On their cursed and mystic pages,
Representing me and mine!
By Tonatiu's fiery shrine!

"When the grass shall grow untrodden
In my war-path, and the plough
Shall be grinding through this canôn
Where my braves are gather'd now,
Still shall they record this vow.

"War and vengeance! rise, my warriors,
Rise and shout the battle-sign,
Ye who love revenge and glory!
Ye for peace, in silence pine,
And no more be braves of mine."

Then the war-yell roll'd and echoed
As they started from the ground,

Till an eagle from his cedar
Starting answer'd back the sound,
And flew circling round and round.

"Enough, enough, my kingly father!"
And the glory of her eyes
Flash'd the valor and the passion
That may sleep but never dies,
As she proudly thus replies:

"Shall the red-wood be a willow,
Pliant and as little worth?
It shall stand the king of forests,
Or its fall shall shake the earth,
Desolating heart and hearth!"

    *   *   *   *   *

    *   *   *   *   *

III.

FROM cold east shore to warm west sea
The red men follow'd the red sun,
And faint and failing fast as he,
Felt, sure as his, their race was run.

This ancient tribe, press'd to the wave,
There fain had slept a patient slave,
And died out as red embers die
From flames that once leapt hot and high;
But, roused to anger, half arose
Around that chief, a sudden flood,
At hot and hungry cry for blood;
Half drowsy shook a feeble hand,
Then sank back in a tame repose,
And left him to his fate and foes,
A stately wreck upon the strand.
His eye was like the lightning's wing,
His voice was like a rushing flood;
He boasted Montezuma's blood,
And when a captive bound he stood
His presence look'd the perfect king.

'Twas held at first that he should die:
I never knew the reason why
A milder council did prevail,
Save that we shrank from blood, and save
That brave men do respect the brave.
Down sea sometimes there was a sail,
And far at sea, they said, an isle,
And he was sentenced to exile,

In open boat upon the sea
To go the instant on the main,
And never under penalty
Of death, to touch the shore again.
A troop of bearded buckskinn'd men
Bore him hard-hurried to the wave,
Placed him swift in the boat; and when
Swift pushing to the bristling sea,
His daughter rush'd down suddenly,
Threw him his bow, leapt from the shore
Into the boat beside the brave,
And sat her down and seized the oar,
And never question'd, made replies,
Or moved her lips, or raised her eyes.

His breast was like a gate of brass,
His brow was like a gather'd storm;
There is no chisell'd stone that has
So stately and complete a form,
In sinew, arm, and every part,
In all the galleries of art.

Grey, bronzed, and naked to the waist,
He stood half halting in the prow,
With quiver bare and idle bow.

His daughter sat with her sad face
Bent on the wave, with her two hands
Held tightly to the dripping oar;
And as she sat, her dimpled knee
Bent lithe as wand of willow tree,
So round and full, so rich and free,
That no one would have ever known
That it had either joint or bone.
The warm sea fondled with the shore,
And laid his white face on the sands.

Her eyes were black, her face was brown,
Her breasts were bare and there fell down
Such wealth of hair, it almost hid
The two, in its rich jetty fold—
Which I had sometime fain forbid,
They were so richer, fuller far
Than any polish'd bronzes are,
And richer hued than any gold.
On her brown arms and her brown hands
Were hoops of gold and golden bands,
Rough hammer'd from the virgin ore,
So heavy, they could hold no more.

I wonder now, I wonder'd then,

That men who fear'd not gods nor men
Laid no rude hand at all on her,
I think she had a dagger slid
Down in her silver'd wampum belt;
It might have been, instead of hilt,
A flashing diamond hurry-hid
That I beheld—I could not know
For certain, we did hasten so;
And I know now less sure than then,
Deeds strangle memories of deeds,
Red blossoms wither, choked with weeds,
And floods drown memories of men.
Some things have happened since—and then
This happen'd years and years ago.

"Go, go!" the captain cried, and smote
With sword and boot the swaying boat,
Until it quiver'd as at sea
And brought the old chief to his knee.
He turn'd his face, and turning rose
With hand raised fiercely to his foes:
"Yes, we will go, last of my race,
Push'd by the robbers ruthlessly
Into the hollows of the sea,
From this the last, last resting-place.

Traditions of my Fathers say
A feeble few reach'd for the land,
And we reach'd them a welcome hand,
Of old, upon another shore;
Now they are strong, we weak as they,
And they have driven us before
Their faces, from that sea to this:
Then marvel not if we have sped
Sometime an arrow as we fled,
So keener than a serpent's kiss."

He turn'd a time unto the sun
That lay half hidden in the sea,
As in his hollows rock'd asleep,
All trembled and breathed heavily;
Then arch'd his arm, as you have done,
For sharp masts piercing through the deep.
No shore or tall ship met the eye,
Or isle, or sail, or anything,
Save white sea-gulls on dipping wing,
And mobile sea and molten sky.

"Farewell!—push   seaward, child!" he
        cried,
And quick the paddle-strokes replied.

Like lightning from the panther-skin,
That bound his loins round about
He snatch'd a poison'd arrow out,
That like a snake lay hid within,
And twang'd his bow. The captain fell
Prone on his face, and such a yell
Of triumph from that savage rose
As man may never hear again.
He stood as standing on the main,
The topmast main, in proud repose,
And shook his clench'd fist at his foes,
And call'd, and cursed them every one.
He heeded not the shouts and shot
That follow'd him, but grand and grim
Stood up against the level sun;
And, standing so, seem'd in his ire
So grander than a leaping fire.

And when the sun had left the sea,
That laves Abrep, and Blanco laves,
And left the land to death and me,
The only thing that I could see
Was, ever as the light boat lay
High lifted on the white-back'd waves,
A head as grey and toss'd as they.

We raised the dead, and from his hands
Pick'd out some shells, clutch'd as he lay
And two by two bore him away,
And wiped his lips of blood and sands.
We bent and scoop'd a shallow home,
And laid him warm-wet in his blood,
Just as the lifted tide a-flood
Came charging in with mouth a-foam:
And as we turn'd, the sensate thing
Reached up, lick'd out its foamy tongue,
Lick'd out its tongue and tasted blood;
The white lips to the red earth clung
An instant, and then loosening
All hold just like a living thing,
Drew back sad-voiced and shuddering,
All stained with blood, a stripéd flood.

THE TALE OF THE TALL ALCALDE.

SHADOWS *that shroud the to-morrow,*
   Glists from the life that's within,
Traces of pain and of sorrow,
   And maybe a trace of sin,
Reachings for God in the darkness,
   And for—what should have been.

Stains from the gall and the wormwood,
   Memories bitter like myrrh,
A sad, brown face in a fir-wood,
   Blotches of heart's blood here,
But never the sound of the wailing,
   Never the sign of a tear.

———

Thou Italy of the Occident!
Land of flowers and summer climes,
Of holy priests and horrid crimes;
Land of the cactus and sweet cocoa;
Richer than all the Orient
In gold and glory, in want and woe
In self-denial, in days misspent,
In truth and treason, in good and guilt,
In ivied ruins and altars low,
In batter'd walls and blood misspilt;
Glorious, gory Mexico!

WHERE mountains repose in their blue-
       ness,
Where the sun first lands in his newness,
And marshals his beams and his lances,
Ere down to the vale he advances
With visor erect, and rides swiftly
On the terrible night in his way,
And slays him, and, daring and deftly,
Hews the beautiful day
With his flashing sword of silver,—
Lay nestled the town of Renalda,
Far famed for its famous Alcalde,
The iron judge of the mountain mine,
With the heart like the heart of woman,
And humanity more than human;—
Far famed for its maids and silver,
Rich mines and its mountain wine.

   The feast was full, and the guests afire,
The shaven priest and the portly squire,
The solemn judge and the smiling dandy,
The duke and the don and the commandanté,
All sat, and shouted or sang divine,
Sailing in one great sea of wine;

Till roused, red-crested knight Chanticleer
Answer'd and echo'd their song and cheer.

They boasted of broil, encounter, and battle,
They boasted of maidens most cleverly won,
Boasted of duels most valiantly done,
Of leagues of land and of herds of cattle,
These men at the feast up in fair Renalda.
All boasted but one, the calm Alcalde,
Though hard they press'd from first of the feast,
Press'd commandantè, press'd poet and priest,
And steadily still the attorney press'd,
With lifted glass and his face aglow,
Heedless of host and careless of guest—
"A tale! the tale of your life, so ho!
For not one man in all Mexico
Can trace your history a half decade."
A hand on the rude one's lips was laid:
"Sacred, my son," a priest went on,
"Sacred the secrets of every one,
Inviolate as an altar-stone.
But what in the life of one who must
Have lived a life that is half divine—
Have been so pure to be so just,
What can there be, O advocate,

In the life of one so desolate
Of luck with matron, or love with maid,
Midnight revel or escapade,
To stir the wonder of men at wine?
But should the Alcalde choose, you know,"—
(And here his voice fell soft and low,
As he set his wine-horn in its place,
And look'd in the judge's careworn face)—
" To weave us a tale that points a moral,
Out of his vivid imagination,
Of lass or of love, or lover's quarrel,
Naught of his fame or name or station
Shall lose in luster by its relation."

Softly the judge set down his horn,
Kindly look'd on the priests all shorn,
And gazed in the eyes of the advocate
With a touch of pity, but none of hate;
Then look'd down into the brimming horn,
Half defiant and half forlorn.

Was it a tear? Was it a sigh?
Was it a glance of the priest's black eye?
Or was it the drunken revel-cry
That smote the rock of his frozen heart

And forced his pallid lips apart?
Or was it the weakness like to woman
Yearning for sympathy
Through the dark years,
Spurning the secrecy,
Burning for tears,
Proving him human,—
As he said to the men of the silver mine,
With their eyes held up as to one divine,
With his eyes held down to his untouch'd wine:

"It might have been where moonbeams
    kneel
At night beside some rugged steep;
It might have been where breakers reel,
Or mild waves cradle men to sleep;
It might have been in peaceful life,
Or mad tumult and storm and strife,
I drew my breath; it matters not.
A silver'd head, a sweetest cot,
A sea of tamarack and pine,
A peaceful stream, a balmy clime,
A cloudless sky, a sister's smile,
A mother's love that sturdy Time
Has strengthen'd as he strengthens wine,

Are mine, are with me all the while,
Are hung in memory's sounding halls,
Are graven on her glowing walls.
But rage, nor rack, nor wrath of man,
Nor prayer of priest, nor price, nor ban
Can wring from me their place or name,
Or why, or when, or whence I came;
Or why I left that childhood home,
A child of form yet old of soul,
And sought the wilds where tempests roll
Round mountains white as driven foam.

" Mistaken and misunderstood,
I sought a deeper wild and wood,
A girlish form and a childish face,
A wild waif drifting from place to place.

" Oh for the skies of rolling blue,
The balmy hours when lovers woo,
When the moon is doubled as in desire,
And the lone bird cries in his crest of fire,
Like vespers calling the soul to bliss
In the blessed love of the life above.
Ere it has taken the stains of this!

" The world afar, yet at my feet,

Went steadily and sternly on;
I almost fancied I could meet
The crush and bustle of the street,
When from the mountain I look'd down.
And deep down in the canon's mouth
The long-tom ran and pick-axe rang,
And pack-trains coming from the south
Went stringing round the mountain high
In long grey lines, as wild geese fly,
While mul'teers shouted hoarse and high,
And dusty, dusky mul'teers sang—
'Senora with the liquid eye!
No floods can ever quench the flame,
Or frozen snows my passion tame,
O Jouana with the coal-black eye!
O senorita, bide a bye!'

"Environ'd by a mountain wall,
That caped in snowy turrets stood;
So fierce, so terrible, so tall,
It never yet had been defiled
By track or trail, save by the wild
Free children of the wildest wood.
An unkiss'd virgin at my feet,
Lay my pure, hallow'd, dreamy vale,

7

Where breathed the essence of my tale;
Lone dimple in the mountain's face,
Lone Eden in a boundless waste
It lay so beautiful! so sweet!

    " There in the sun's decline I stood
By God's form wrought in pink and pearl,
My peerless, dark-eyed Indian girl;
And gazed out from a fringe of wood,
With full-fed soul and feasting eyes,
Upon an earthly paradise.
Inclining to the south it lay,
And long league's southward roll'd away,
Until the sable-feather'd pines
And tangled boughs and amorous vines
Closed like besiegers on the scene,
The while the stream that intertwined
Had barely room to flow between.
It was unlike all other streams,
Save those seen in sweet summer dreams;
For sleeping in its bed of snow,
Nor rock nor stone was ever known,
But only shining, shifting sands,
Forever sifted by unseen hands.
It curved, it bent like Indian bow,

And like an arrow darted through,
Yet uttered not a sound nor breath,
Nor broke a ripple from the start;
It was as swift, as still as death,
Yet was so clear, so pure, so sweet,
It wound its way into your heart
As through the grasses at your feet.

"Once, through the tall untangled grass,
I saw two black bears careless pass,
And in the twilight turn to play;
I caught my rifle to my face,
She raised her hand with quiet grace
And said, 'Not so, for us the day,
The night belongs to such as they.'

"And then from out the shadow'd wood
The antler'd deer came stalking down
In half a shot of where I stood;
Then stopp'd and stamp'd impatiently,
Then shook his head and antlers high,
And then his keen horns backward threw
Upon his shoulders broad and brown,
And thrust his muzzle in the air,
Snuff'd proudly; then a blast he blew

As if to say, " No danger here."
And then from out the sable wood
His mate and two sweet dappled fawns
Stole forth, and by the monarch stood,
She timid, while the little ones
Would start like aspens in a gale.
Then he, as if to reassure
The timid, trembling and demure,
Again his antlers backward threw,
Again a blast defiant blew,
Then led them proudly down the vale.

" I watch'd the forms of darkness come
Slow stealing from their sylvan home,
And pierce the sunlight drooping low
And weary, as if loth to go.
He stain'd the lances as he bled,
And, bleeding and pursued, he fled
Across the vale into the wood.
I saw the tall grass bend its head
Beneath the stately martial tread
Of Shades, pursuer and pursued.

"'Behold the clouds,' Winnema said,
'All purple with the blood of day;

The night has conquer'd in the fray,
The shadows live, and light is dead.'

  " She turn'd to Shasta gracefully,
Around whose hoar and mighty head
Still roll'd a sunset sea of red,
While troops of clouds a space below
Were drifting wearily and slow,
As seeking shelter for the night,
Like weary sea-birds in their flight;
Then curved her right arm gracefully
Above her brow, and bow'd her knee,
And chanted in an unknown tongue
Words sweeter than were ever sung.

  " ' And what means this?' I gently said.
' I spoke to God, the Yopitone,
Who dwells on yonder snowy throne,'
She softly said with drooping head;
' I bow'd to God. He heard my prayer,
I felt his warm breath in my hair,
He heard me all my desires tell,
And He is good, and all is well.'

  " The dappled and the dimpled skies,
The timid stars, the tinted moon,

All smiled as sweet as sun at noon.
Her eyes were like the rabbit's eyes,
Her mien, her manner, just as mild,
And though a savage war-chief's child,
She would not harm the lowliest worm.
And, though her beaded foot was firm,
And though her airy step was true,
She would not crush a drop of dew.

    " Her love was deeper than the sea,
And stronger than the tidal rise,
And clung in all its strength to me.
A face like hers is never seen
This side the gates of paradise,
Save in some Indian-Summer scene,
And then none ever sees it twice—
Is seen but once, and seen no more,
Seen but to tempt the sceptic soul,
And show a sample of the whole
That Heaven has in store.

    "You might have plucked beams from the
        moon,
Or torn the shadow from the pine
When on its dial track at noon,

But not have parted us an hour,
She was so wholly, truly mine.
And life was one unbroken dream
Of purest bliss and calm delight,
A flow'ry-shored, untroubled stream
Of sun and song, of shade and bower,
A full-moon'd serenading night.

" Sweet melodies were in the air,
And tame birds caroll'd everywhere.
I listened to the lisping grove
And cooing pink-eyed turtle dove,
And loving with the holiest love,
Believing with a grand belief
That everything beneath the skies
Was beautiful and born to love,
That man had but to love, believe,
And earth would be a paradise
As beautiful as that above.
My goddess, Beauty, I adored,
Devoutly, fervid, her alone;
My Priestess, Love, unceasing pour'd
Pure incense on her altar-stone.

" I carved my name in coarse design

Once on a birch down by the way,
At which she gazed, as she would say,
'What does this say? What is this sign?'
And when I gaily said, 'Some day
Some one will come and read my name,
And I will live in song and fame,
Entwined with many a mountain tale,
As he who first found this sweet vale,
And they will give the place my name,'
She was most sad, and troubled much,
And looked in silence far away;
Then started trembling from my touch,
And when she turn'd her face again,
I read unutterable pain.

  "At last she answered through her tears,
' Ah! yes; this, too, fulfils my fears.
Yes, they will come—my race must go
As fades a vernal fall of snow;
And you be known, and I forgot
Like these brown leaves that rust and rot
Beneath my feet; and it is well:
I do not seek to thrust my name
On those who here, hereafter, dwell,
Because I have before them dwelt;

They too will have their tales to tell,
They too will ask their time and fame.

  " 'Yes, they will come, come even now:
The dim ghosts on yon mountain's brow,
Grey Fathers of my tribe and race,
Do beckon to us from their place,
And hurl red arrows through the air
At night, to bid our braves beware.
A footprint by the clear McCloud,
Unlike aught ever seen before,
Is seen.   The crash of rifles loud
Is heard along its farther shore.'

           *   *   *   *   *

  "What tall and tawny men were these,
As sombre, silent, as the trees
They moved among! and sad some way
With temper'd sadness, ever they,—
Yet not with sorrow born of fear.
The shadow of their destinies
They saw approaching year by year,
And murmur'd not.   They saw the sun
Go down; they saw the peaceful moon
Move on in silence to her rest,
And white streams winding to the west:

And thus they knew that oversoon,
Somehow, somewhere, for every one
Was rest beyond the setting sun.
They knew not, never dream'd of doubt,
But turn'd to death as to a sleep,
And died with eager hands held out
To reaching hands beyond the deep,—
And died with choicest bow at hand,
And quiver full, and arrow drawn
For use, when sweet to-morrow's dawn
Should wake them in the Spirit Land.

"What wonder that I linger'd there
With Nature's children! Could I part
With those that met me heart to heart,
And made me welcome, spoke me fair
Were first of all that understood
My waywardness from other's ways,
My worship of the true and good,
And earnest love of Nature's God?
Go court the mountains in the clouds,
And clashing thunder, and the shrouds
Of tempests, and eternal shocks,
And fast and pray as one of old
In earnestness, and ye shall hold

The mysteries; shall hold the rod
That passes seas, that smites the rocks
Where streams of melody and song
Shall run as white streams rush and flow
Down from the mountains' crests of snow,
Forever, to a thirsting throng.

*　　*　　*　　*　　*

"Between the white man and the red
There lies no neutral, half-way ground.
I heard afar the thunder sound
That soon should burst above my head,
And made my choice; I laid my plan,
And child-like chose the weaker side;
And ever have, and ever will,
While might is wrong and wrongs remain,
As careless of the world as I
Am careless of a cloudless sky.
With wayward and romantic joy
I gave my pledge like any boy,
But kept my promise like a man,
And lost; yet with the lesson still
Would gladly do the same again.

"'They come! they come! the pale-face
    come!'

The chieftain shouted where he stood,
Sharp watching at the margin wood,
And gave the war-whoop's treble yell,
That like a knell on fond hearts fell
Far watching from the rocky home.

" No nodding plumes or banners fair
Unfurl'd or fretted through the air;
No screaming fife or rolling drum
Did challenge brave of soul to come:
But, silent, sinew-bows were strung,
And, sudden, heavy quivers hung,
And, swiftly, to the battle sprung
Tall painted braves with tufted hair,
Like death-black banners in the air.

"And long they fought, and firm and well
And silent fought, and silent fell,
Save when they gave the fearful yell
Of death, defiance, or of hate,
But what were feather'd flints to fate?
And what were yells to seething lead?
And what the few and feeble feet
To troops that came with martial tread,
And moved by wood and hill and stream

As thick as people in a street,
As strange as spirits in a dream?

"From pine and poplar, here and there,
A cloud, a flash, a crash, a thud,
A warrior's garments roll'd in blood,
A yell that rent the mountain air
Of fierce defiance and despair,
Did tell who fell, and when and where.
Then tighter drew the coils around,
And closer grew the battle-ground,
And fewer feather'd arrows fell,
And fainter grew the battle yell,
Until upon the hill was heard
The short, sharp whistle of the bird.

"The calm, that cometh after all,
Look'd sweetly down at shut of day,
Where friend and foe commingled lay
Like leaves of forest as they fall.
Afar the somber mountains frown'd,
Here tall pines wheel'd their shadows round,
Like long, slim fingers of a hand
That sadly pointed out the dead.
Like some broad shield high overhead

The great white moon led on and on,
As leading to the better land.
You might have heard the cricket's trill,
Or night-birds calling from the hill,
The place was so profoundly still.

"The mighty chief at last was down,
A broken gate of brass and pride!
The hair all dust, and this his crown!
His firm lips were compress'd in hate
To foes, yet all content with fate;
While, circled round him thick, the foe
Had folded hands in dust, and died.
His tomahawk lay at his side,
All blood, beside his broken bow.
One arm stretch'd out as over-bold,
One hand half doubled hid in dust,
And clutch'd the earth, as if to hold
His hunting grounds still in his trust.

"Here tall grass bow'd its tassel'd head
In dewy tears above the dead,
And there they lay in crook'd fern,
That waved and wept above by turn:
And further on, by somber trees,

They lay, wild heroes of wild deeds,
In shrouds alone of weeping weeds,
Bound in a never-to-be-broken peace.

"Not one had falter'd, not one brave
Survived the fearful struggle, save
One—save I the renegade,
The red man's friend, and—they held me so
For this alone—the white man's foe.

"They bore me bound for many a day
Through fen and wild, by foamy flood,
From my dear mountains far away,
Where an adobé prison stood
Beside a sultry sullen, town,
With iron eyes and stony frown;
And in a dark and narrow cell,
So hot it almost took my breath,
And seem'd but some outpost of hell,
They thrust me—as if I had been
A monster, in a monster's den.
I cried aloud, I courted death,
I call'd unto a strip of sky,
The only thing beyond my cell
That I could see, but no reply

Came but the echo of my breath.
I paced—how long I cannot tell—
My reason fail'd, I knew no more,
And swooning fell upon the floor.
Then months went on, till deep one night,
When long thin bars of cool moonlight
Lay shimmering along the floor,
My senses came to me once more.

"My eyes look'd full into her eyes—
Into her soul so true and tried.
I thought myself in paradise,
And wonder'd when she too had died.
And then I saw the stripéd light
That struggled past the prison bar,
And in an instant, at the sight,
My sinking soul fell just as far
As could a star loosed by a jar
From out the setting in a ring,
The purpled semi-circled ring
That seems to circle us at night.

" She saw my senses had return'd,
Then swift to press my pallid face—
Then, as if spurn'd, she sudden turn'd

Her sweet face to the prison wall;
Her bosom rose, her hot tears fell
Fast as drip moss-stones in a well,
And then, as if subduing all
In one strong struggle of the soul,
Be what they were of vows or fears,
With kisses and hot tender tears,
There in that deadly, loathsome place,
She bathed my pale and piteous face.

" I was so weak I could not speak
Or press my pale lips to her cheek;
I only looked my wish to share
The secret of her presence there.
Then looking through her falling hair,
She press'd her finger to her lips,
More sweet than sweets the brown bee sips.
More sad than any grief untold,
More silent than the milk-white moon,
She turned away.   I heard unfold
An iron door, and she was gone.

" At last, one midnight, I was free;
Again I felt the liquid air
Around my hot brow like a sea,

8

Sweet as my dear Madonna's prayer,
Or benedictions on the soul;
Pure air, which God gives free to all,
Again I breathed without control—
Pure air that man would fain enthral;
God's air, which man hath seized and **sold**
Unto his fellow-man for gold.

" I bow'd down to the bended sky,
I toss'd my two thin hands on high,
I call'd unto the crooked moon,
I shouted to the shining stars,
With breath and rapture uncontroll'd,
Like some wild school-boy loosed at **noon,**
Or comrade coming from the wars,
Hailing his companeers of old.

" Short time for shouting or delay,—
The cock is shrill, the east is **grey,**
Pursuit is made, I must **away.**
They cast me on a sinewy steed,
And bid me look to girth and guide—
A caution of but little need.
I dash the iron in his side,
Swift as the shooting stars I ride;

I turn, I see, to my dismay,
A silent rider red as they;
I glance again—it is my bride,
My love, my life, rides at my side.

" By gulch and gorge and brake and all,
Swift as the shining meteors fall,
We fly, and never sound nor word
But ringing mustang-hoofs is heard,
And limbs of steel and lungs of steam
Could not be stronger than theirs seem.
Grandly as some joyous dream,
League on league, and hour on hour,
Far from keen pursuit, or power
Of sheriff or bailiff, high or low,
Into the bristling hills we go.

" Into the tumbled, clear McCloud,
White as the foldings of a shroud;
We dash into the dashing stream,
We breast the tide, we drop the rein,
We clutch the streaming, tangled mane—
And yet the rider at my side
Has never look nor word replied.

"Out in its foam, its rush, its roar,

Breasting away to the farther shore;
Steadily, bravely, gain'd at last,
Gain'd, where never a dastard foe
Has dared to come, or friend to go.
Pursuit is baffled and danger pass'd.

"Under an oak whose wide arms were
Lifting aloft, as if in prayer,
Under an oak, where the shining moon
Like feather'd snow in a winter noon
Quiver'd, sifted, and drifted down
In spars and bars on her shoulders brown:
And yet she was as silent still
As black stones toppled from the hill—
Great basalt blocks that near us lay,
Deep nestled in the grass untrod
By aught save wild beasts of the wood—
Great, massive, squared, and chisel'd stone,
Like columns that had toppled down
From temple dome or tower crown.
Along some drifted, silent way
Of desolate and desert town
Built by the children of the sun.
And I in silence sat on one,
And she stood gazing far away

To where her childhood forests lay,
Still as the stone I sat upon.

"I sought to catch her to my breast
And charm her from her silent mood;
She shrank as if a beam, a breath,
Then silently before me stood,
Still, coldly, as the kiss of death.
Her face was darker than a pall,
Her presence was so proudly tall,
I would have started from the stone
Where I sat gazing up at her,
As from a form to earth unknown,
Had I possess'd the power to stir.

"'O touch me not, no more, no more;
'Tis past, and my sweet dream is o'er.
Impure! Impure! Impure!" she cried,
In words as sweetly, weirdly wild
As mingling of a rippled tide,
And music on the waters spill'd. . . .
'But you are free. Fly! Fly alone.
Yes, you will win another bride
In some far clime where naught is known
Of all that you have won or lost,
Or what your life this night has cost;

Will win you name, and place, and power,
And ne'er recall this face, this hour,
Save in some secret, deep regret,
Which I forgive and you'll forget.
Your destiny will lead you on
Where, open'd wide to welcome you,
Rich, ardent hearts and bosoms are,
And snowy arms, more purely fair,
And breasts—who dare say breasts more true?

"'They said you had deserted me,
Had rued you of your wood and wild.
I knew, I knew it could not be,
I trusted as a trusting child.
I cross'd the bristled mountain high
That curves its rough back to the sky,
I rode the white-maned mountain flood,
And track'd for weeks the trackless wood.
The good God led me, as before,
And brought me to your prison-door.

"'That madden'd call! that fever'd moan!
I heard you in the midnight call
My own name through the massive wall,
In my sweet mountain-tongue and tone—

And yet you call'd so feebly wild,
I near mistook you for a child.

The keeper with his clinking keys
I sought, implored upon my knees
That I might see you, feel your breath,
Your brow, or breathe you low replies
Of comfort in your lonely death.
His red face shone, his redder eyes
Were like the fire of the skies;
Then all his face was as a fire,
As he said, "Yield to my desire."
Again I heard your feeble moan,
I cried, "And must he die alone?"
I cried unto a heart of stone.
Ah! why the hateful horrors tell?
Enough! I crept into your cell.

"'I nursed you, lured you back to life,
And when you woke and call'd me wife
And love, with pale lips rife
With love and feeble loveliness,
I turn'd away, I hid my face,
In mad reproach and deep distress,
In dust down in that loathsome place.

"'And then I vow'd a solemn vow
That you should live, live and be free.
And you have lived—are free; and now
Too slow yon red sun comes to see
My life or death, or me again.
Oh, death! the peril and the pain
I have endured! the dark, dark stain
That I did take on my fair soul,
All, all to save you, make you free,
Are more than mortal can endure:
But fire makes the foulest pure.

"'Behold this finish'd funeral pyre,
All ready for the form and fire,
Which these, my own hands, did prepare
For this last night; then lay me there.
I would not hide me from my God
Beneath the cold and sullen sod,
But, wrapp'd in fiery shining shroud,
Ascend to Him, a wreathing cloud.'

"She paused, she turn'd, she lean'd apace
Her glance and half-regretting face,
As if to yield herself to me;
And then she cried, 'It cannot be,

For I have vow'd a solemn vow,
And God help me to keep it now!'

"I sprang with arms extended wide
To catch her to my burning breast;
She caught a dagger from her side
And, ere I knew to stir or start,
She plunged it in her bursting heart,
And fell into my arms and died—
Died as my soul to hers was press'd,
Died as I held her to my breast,
Died without one word or moan,
And left me with my dead—alone.

"I laid my dead upon the pile,
And underneath the lisping oak
I watch'd the columns of dark smoke
Embrace her red lips, with a smile
Of frenzied fierceness. Then there came
A gleaming column of red flame,
That grew a grander monument
Above her nameless noble mould
Than ever bronze or marble lent
To king or conqueror of old.

"It seized her in its hot embrace,
And leapt as if to reach the stars.
Then looking up I saw a face
So saintly and so sweetly fair,
So sad, so pitying, and so pure,
I nigh forgot the prison bars,
And for one instant, one alone,
I felt I could forgive, endure.

"I laid a circlet of white stone,
And left her ashes there alone.
But after many a white moon-wane
I sought that sacred ground again.
I saw the circle of white stone
With tall wild grasses overgrown.
I did expect, I know not why,
From out her sacred dust to find
Wild pinks and daisies blooming fair;
And when I did not find them there
I almost deem'd her God unkind,
Less careful of her dust than I.

"But why the dreary tale prolong?
And deem you I confess'd me wrong,
That I did bend a patient knee

To all the deep wrongs done to me?
That I, because the prison mould
Was on my brow, and all its chill
Was in my heart as chill as night,
Till soul and body both were cold,
Did curb my free-born mountain will
And sacrifice my sense of right?

"No! no! and had they come that day
While I with hands and garments red
Stood by her pleading, gory clay,
The one lone watcher by my dead,
With cross-hilt dagger in my hand,
And offer'd me my life and all
Of titles, power, or of place,
I should have spat them in the face,
And spurn'd them every one.
I live as God gave me to live,
I see as God gave me to see.
'Tis not my nature to forgive,
Or cringe and plead and bend the knee
To God or man in woe or weal,
In penitence I cannot feel.

"I do not question school nor creed
Of Christian, Protestant, or Priest;

I only know that creeds to me
Are but new names for mystery,
That God is good from east to east,
And more I do not know nor need
To know, to love my neighbor well.
I take their dogmas, as they tell,
Their pictures of their Godly good,
In garments thick with heathen blood;
Their heaven with its harps of gold,
Their horrid pictures of their hell,
Take hell and heaven undenied,
Yet were the two placed side by side,
Placed full before me for my choice,
As they are pictured, best and worst,
As they are peopled, tame and bold,
The canonized, and the accursed
Who dared to think, and thinking speak,
And speaking act, bold cheek to cheek,
I would in transports choose the first,
And enter hell with lifted voice.

* * * * *

"Go read the annals of the North,
And records there of many a wail,
Of marshalling and going forth
For missing sheriffs, and for men

Who fell and none knew where nor when,—
Who disappear'd on mountain trail,
Or in some dense and narrow vale.
Go, traverse Trinity and Scott,
That curve their dark backs to the sun:
Go, court them all.   Lo! have they not
The chronicles of my wild life?
My secrets on their lips of stone,
My archives built of human bone?
Go, range their wilds as I have done,
From snowy crest to sleeping vales,
And you will find on every one
Enough to swell a thousand tales.

*   *   *   *   *

  "The soul cannot survive alone,
And hate will die, like other things;
I felt an ebbing in my rage,
I hunger'd for the sound of one,
Just one familiar word,—
Yearn'd but to hear my fellow speak,
Or sound of woman's mellow tone,
As beats the wild, imprison'd bird,
That long nor kind nor mate has heard,
With bleeding wings and panting beak
Against its iron cage.

"I saw a low-roof'd rancho lie,
Far, far below, at set of sun,
Along the foot-hills crisp and dun—
A lone sweet star in lower sky;
Saw children sporting to and fro,
The busy housewife come and go,
And white cows come at her command,
And none look'd larger than my hand.
Then worn and torn, and tann'd and brown,
And heedless all, I hasten'd down;
A wanderer wandering long and late,
I stood before the rustic gate.

"Two little girls, with brown feet bare,
And tangled, tossing, yellow hair,
Play'd on the green, fantastic dress'd,
Around a great Newfoundland brute
That lay half-resting on his breast,
And with his red mouth open'd wide
Would make believe that he would bite,
As they assail'd him left and right,
And then sprang to the other side,
And fill'd with shouts the willing air.
Oh, sweeter far than lyre or lute
To my then hot and thirsty heart,

And better self so wholly mute,
Were those sweet voices calling there.

"Though some sweet scenes my eyes have
   seen,
Some melody my soul has heard,
No song of any maid, or bird,
Or splendid wealth of tropic scene,
Or scene or song of anywhere,
Has my impulsive soul so stirr'd,
As those young angels sporting there.

"The dog at sight of me arose,
And nobly stood, with lifted nose,
Afront the children, now so still,
And staring at me with a will.
'Come in, come in,' the rancher cried,
As here and there the housewife hied;
'Sit down, sit down, you travel late.
What news of politics or war?
And are you tired? Go you far?
And where you from? Be quick, my Kate,
This boy is sure in need of food.'
The little children close by stood,
And watch'd and gazed inquiringly,
Then came and climb'd upon my knee.

"'That there's my ma,' the eldest said,
And laugh'd and toss'd her pretty head;
And then, half bating of her joy,
'Have you a ma, you stranger boy?—
And there hangs Carlo on the wall
As large as life; that mother drew
With berry stains upon a shred
Of tattered tent; but hardly you
Would know the picture his at all,
For Carlo's black, and this is red.'
Again she laugh'd, and shook her head,
And shower'd curls all out of place;
Then sudden sad, she raised her face
To mine, and tenderly she said,
'Have you, like us, a pretty home?
Have you, like me, a dog and toy?
Where do you live, and whither roam?
And where's your pa, poor stranger boy?'

"It seem'd so sweetly out of place
Again to meet my fellow-man,
I gazed and gazed upon his face
As something I had never seen.
The melody of woman's voice
Fell on my ear as falls the rain

Upon the weary, waiting plain.
I heard, and drank and drank again,
As earth with crack'd lips drinks the rain,
In green to revel and rejoice.
I ate with thanks my frugal food,
The first return'd for many a day.
I had met kindness by the way!
I had at last encounter'd good!

"I sought my couch, but not to sleep;
New thoughts were coursing strong and deep
My wild, impulsive passion-heart;
I could not rest, my heart was moved,
My iron will forgot its part,
And I wept like a child reproved.

"I lay and pictured me a life
Afar from cold reproach or stain,
Or annals dark of blood and strife,
From deadly perils or heart-pain;
And at the breaking of the morn
I swung my arms from off the horn,
And turned to other scenes and lands
With lighten'd heart and whiten'd hands.

9

"Where orange-blossoms never die,
Where red fruits ripen all the year
Beneath a sweet and balmy sky,
Far from my language or my land,
Reproach, regret, or shame or fear,
I came in hope, I wander'd here—
Yes, here; and this red, bony hand
That holds this glass of ruddy cheer—"

" 'Tis he!" hiss'd the crafty advocate.
He sprang to his feet, and hot with hate
He reach'd his hands, and he call'd aloud,
" 'Tis the renegade of the red McCloud!"

Slowly the Alcade rose from his chair;
"Hand me, touch me, him who dare!"
And his heavy glass on the board of oak
He smote with such savage and mighty stroke,
It ground to dust in his bony hand,
And heavy bottles did clink and tip
As if an earthquake were in the land.
He tower'd up, and in his ire
Seem'd taller than a church's spire.
He gazed a moment—and then, the while
An icy cold and defiant smile

Did curve his thin and his livid lip,
He turn'd on his heel, he stode through the hall
Grand as a god, so grandly tall,
Yet white and cold as a chisel'd stone;
He passed him out the adobe door
Into the night, and he pass'd alone,
And never was known nor heard of more.

A WILD, *wide land of mysteries,*
    Of sea-salt lakes and dried-up seas,
And lonely wells and pools; a land
That seems so like dead Palestine,
Save that its wastes have no confine
Till push'd against the levell'd skies.
A land from out whose depths shall rise
The new-time prophets. Yea, the land
From out whose awful depths shall come,
All clad in skins, with dusty feet,
A man fresh from his Maker's hand,
A singer singing oversweet,
A charmer charming very wise;
And then all men shall not be dumb.
Nay, not be dumb; for he shall say,
"Take heed, for I prepare the way
For weary feet." Lo! from this land
Of Jordan streams and sea-wash'd sand,
The Christ shall come when next the race
Of man shall look upon His face.

THE SHIP IN THE DESERT

I.

A MAN in middle Aridzone
    Stood by the desert's edge alone,
And long he look'd, and lean'd, and peer'd,
And twirl'd about his twisted beard,

Beneath a black and slouchy hat—
Nay, nay, the tale is not of that.

A skin-clad trapper, toe-a-tip,
Stood on a mountain top; and he
Look'd long, and still, and eagerly.
" It looks so like some lonesome ship
That sails this ghostly, lonely sea,—
This dried-up desert sea," said he,
" These tawny sands of Arazit." . . .
Avaunt! this tale is not of it.

A chief from out the desert's rim
Rode swift as twilight swallows swim.
A wild and wiry man was he,
This tawny chief of Shoshonee;
And O!his supple steed was fleet!
About his breast flapp'd panther skins,
About his eager flying feet
Flapp'd beaded, braided moccasins:
He stopp'd, he stood as still as stone,
He lean'd, he look'd, there glisten'd bright,
From out the yellow, yielding sand,
A golden cup with jewell'd rim.
He lean'd him low, he reach'd a hand.

He caught it up, he gallop'd on,
He turn'd his head, he saw a sight. . . .
His panther-skins flew to the wind,
He rode into the rim of night;
The dark, the desert lay behind;
The tawny Ishmaelite was gone.

He reach'd the town, and there held up
Above his head a jewel'd cup.
He put two fingers to his lip,
He whisper'd wild, he stood a-tip,
And lean'd the while with lifted hand,
And said, " A ship lies yonder dead,"
And said, " Doubloons lie sown in sand
In yon far desert dead and brown,
Beyond where wave-wash'd walls look down,
As thick as stars set overhead."
"'Tis from that desert ship," they said,
"That sails with neither sail nor breeze,
The lonely bed of dried-up seas,—
A galleon that sank below
Dead seas ere yet we drew the bow."

By Arizona's sea of sand
Some bearded miners, grey and old,

And resolute in search of gold,
Sat down to tap the savage land.
A miner stood beside his mine,
He pull'd his beard, then looked away
Across the level sea of sand,
Beneath his broad and hairy hand,
A hand as hard of knots of pine.
"It looks so like a sea," said he.
He pull'd his beard, and he did say,
"It looks just like a dried-up sea."
Again he pull'd that beard of his,
But said no other thing than this.

The stalwart miner dealt a stroke,
And struck a buried beam of oak.
The miner twisted, twirl'd his beard,
Lean'd on his pickaxe as he spoke:
"'Tis from some long-lost ship," he said,
"Some laden ship of Solomon
That sail'd these lonesome seas upon
In search of Ophir's mine, ah me!
That sail'd this dried-up desert sea."....
Nay, nay, 'tis not a tale of gold,
But ghostly land, storm-slain and old.

II.

And this the tale.   Along a wide
And sounding stream some silent braves,
That stole along the farther side
Through sweeping wood that swept the waves
Like long arms reach'd across the tide,
Kept watch and every foe defied.

A low, black boat that hugg'd the shores,
An ugly boat, an ugly crew,
Thick-lipp'd and woolly-headed slaves,
That bow'd, and bent the white-ash oars,
That cleft the murky waters through,
Slow climb'd the swift Missouri's waves.

A grand old Neptune in the prow,
Grey-hair'd, and white with touch of time,
Yet strong as in his middle prime,
Stood up, turn'd suddenly, look'd back
Along his low boat's wrinkled track,
Then drew his mantle round, and now
He sat all silently.   Beside
The grim old sea-king sat his bride,

A sun-land blossom, rudely torn
From tropic forests to be worn
Above as stern a breast as e'er
Stood king at sea, or anywhere.

Another boat with other crew
Came swift and cautious in her track,
And now shot shoreward, now shot back,
And now sat rocking fro and to,
But never once lost sight of her.
Tall, sunburnt, southern men were these
From isles of blue Caribbean seas,
And one, that woman's worshipper,
Who look'd on her, and loved but her.

And one, that one, was wild as seas
That wash the far, dark Oregon.
And one, that one, had eyes to teach
The art of love, and tongue to preach
Life's hard and sober homilies,
While he stood leaning, urging on.

III.

Pursuer and pursued. And who
Are these that make the sable crew;

These mighty Titans, black and nude,
And hairy-breasted, bronzed and broad
Of chest as any demi-god,
That dare this peopled solitude?

And who is he that leads them here,
And breaks the hush of wave and wood?
Comes he for evil or for good?
Brave Jesuit or bold buccaneer?

Nay, these be idle themes.   Let pass.
These be but men.   We may forget
The wild sea-king, the tawny brave,
The frowning wold, the woody shore,
The tall-built, sunburnt men of Mars.
But what and who was she, the fair?
The fairest face that ever yet
Look'd in a wave as in a glass;
That look'd as look the still, far stars,
So woman-like, into the wave
To contemplate their beauty there?

I only saw her, heard the sound
Of murky waters gurgling round
In counter-currents from the shore,

But heard the long, strong stroke of oar
Against the waters grey and vast;
I only saw her as she pass'd—
A great, sad beauty, in whose eyes
Lay all the loves of Paradise....

O you had loved her sitting there,
Half hidden in her loosen'd hair;
Yea, loved her for her large dark eyes,
Her push'd out mouth, her mute surprise—
Her mouth! 'twas Egypt's mouth of old,
Push'd out and pouting full and bold
With simple beauty where she sat.
Why, you had said, on seeing her,
This creature comes from out the dim,
Far centuries, beyond the rim
Of time's remotest reach or stir;
And he who wrought Semiramis
And shaped the Sibyls, seeing this,
Had bow'd and made a shrine thereat,
And all his life had worshipp'd her.

IV.

The black men bow'd, the long oars bent,
They struck as if for sweet life's sake,

And one look'd back, but no man spake,
And all wills bent to one intent.

On, through the golden fringe of day
Into the deep, dark night, away
And up the wave 'mid walls of wood
They cleft, they climb'd, they bow'd, they
    bent,
But one stood tall, and restless stood,
And one sat still all night, all day,
And gazed in helpless wonderment.

Her hair pour'd down like darkling wine,
The black men lean'd a sullen line,
The bent oars kept a steady song,
And all the beams of bright sunshine
That touch'd the waters wild and strong,
Fell drifting down and out of sight
Like fallen leaves, and it was night.

And night and day, and many days
They climb'd the sudden, dark grey tide.
And she sat silent at his side,
And he sat turning many ways:

Sat watching for his wily foe;
At last he baffled him. And yet
His brow gloom'd dark, his lips were set;
He lean'd, he peer'd through boughs, as though
From heart of forests deep and dim
Grim shapes could come confronting him.

A grand, uncommon man was he,
Broad-shoulder'd, as of Gothic form,
Strong-built, and hoary like a sea;
A high sea broken up by storm.
His face was brown and over-wrought
By seams and shadows born of thought,
Not over-gentle. And his eyes,
Bold, restless, resolute and deep,
Too deep to flow like shallow fount
Of common men where waters mount;—
Fierce, lumined eyes, where flames might rise
Instead of flood, and flash and sweep—
Strange eyes, that look'd unsatisfied
With all things fair or otherwise;
As if his inmost soul had cried
All time for something yet unseen,
Some long-desiréd thing denied.

V.

Below the overhanging boughs
The oars lay idle at the last;
Yet long he look'd for hostile prows
From out the wood and down the stream.
They came not, and he came to dream
Pursuit abandon'd, danger past.

He fell'd the oak, he built a home
Of new-hewn wood with busy hand,
And said, "My wanderings are told,"
And said, "No more by sea, by land,
Shall I break rest, or drift, or roam,
For I am worn, and I grow old."

And there, beside that surging tide,
Where grey waves meet, and wheel, and strike,
The man sat down as satisfied
To sit and rest unto the end;
As if the strong man here had found
A sort of brother in the sea,—
This surging, sounding majesty
Of troubled water, so profound,

So sullen, strong, and lion-like,
So sinuous and foamy bound.

Hast seen Missouri cleave the wood
In sounding whirlpools to the sea?
What soul hath known such majesty?
What man stood by and understood?

VI.

Then long the long oars idle lay.
The cabin's smoke came forth and curl'd
Right lazily from river brake,
And Time went by the other way.
And who was she, the strong man's pride,
This one fair woman of his world,
A captive? Bride, or not a bride?
Her eyes, men say, grew sad and dim
With watching from the river's rim,
As waiting for some face denied.

Yea, who was she?—none ever knew.
The great, strong river swept around,
The cabins nestled in its bend,

But kept its secrets.   Wild birds flew
In bevies by.   The black men found
Diversion in the chase: and wide
Old Morgan ranged the wood, nor friend
Nor foeman ever sought his side,
Or shared his forests deep and dim,
Or cross'd his path or question'd him.

He stood as one who found and named
The middle world.   What visions flamed
Athwart the west! What prophecies ·
Were his, the grey old man, that day
Who stood alone and look'd away,—
Awest from out the waving trees,
Against the utter sundown seas.

Alone ofttime beside the stream
He stood and gazed as in a dream,—
As if he knew a life unknown
To those who knew him thus alone.
His eyes were grey and overborne
By shaggy brows, his strength was shorn,
Yet still he ever gazed awest,
As one that would not, could not rest

And whence came he? and when and why?
Men question'd men, but naught was known
Save that he roam'd the woods alone,
And lived alone beneath the stir
Of leaves, and letting life go by,
Did look on her and only her.

And had he fled with bloody hand?
Or had he loved some Helen fair,
And battling lost both land and town?
Say, did he see his walls go down,
Then choose from all his treasures there
This love, and seek some other land?

VII.

The squirrels chatter'd in the leaves,
The turkeys call'd from pawpaw wood,
The deer with lifted nostrils stood,
And humming-birds did wind and weave,
Swim round about, dart in and out,
Through fragrant forest hedge made red,
Made many-color'd overhead
By climbing blossoms sweet with bee
And snow-white rose of Cherokee.
10

The frosts came by and touch'd the leaves,
Then time hung ices on the eaves,
Then cushion snows possess'd the ground,
And so the seasons kept their round;
Yet still old Morgan went and came
From cabin door though forest dim,
Through wold of snows, through wood of
        flame,
Through golden Indian-summer days,
Hung round in soft September haze,
And no man cross'd or questioned him.

Nay, there was that in his stern air
That held e'en these rude men aloof:
None came to share the broad-built roof
That rose so fortress-like beside
The angry, rushing, sullen tide,
And only black men gather'd there,
The old man's slaves, in dull content,
Black, silent, and obedient.

Then men push'd westward through his
        wood,
His wild beasts fled, and now he stood
Confronting men. He had endear'd

No man, but still he went and came
Apart, and shook his beard and strode
His ways alone, and bore his load,
If load it were, apart, alone.
Then men grew busy with a name
That no man loved, that many fear'd,
And rude men stoop'd, and cast a stone,
As at some statue overthrown.

Some said a pirate blown by night
From isles of calm Caribbean land,
Who left his comrades; that he fled
With many prices on his head,
And that he bore in his hot flight
The gather'd treasure of his band,
In bloody and unholy hand.

Then some did say a privateer,
Then others, that he fled from fear,
And climb'd the mad Missouri far,
To where the friendly forests are;
And that his illy-gotten gold
Lay sunken in his black boat's hold.
Then others, watching his fair bride,
Said, "There is something more beside."

Some said, a stolen bride was she,
And that her lover from the sea
Lay waiting for his chosen wife,
And that a day of reckoning
Lay waiting for this grizzled king,

VIII.

O dark-eyed Ina!   All the years
Brought her but solitude and tears.
Lo! ever looking out she stood
Adown the wave, adown the wood,
Adown the strong stream to the south,
Sad-faced, and sorrowful.   Her mouth
Push'd out so pitiful.   Her eyes
Fill'd full of sorrow, or surprise.
O sweet child-face, that ever gazed
From out the wood and down the wave
O eyes, that never once were raised!
O mouth, that never murmur gave!

Men say that looking from her place
A love would sometimes light her face,
As if sweet recollections stirr'd
Her heart and broke its loneliness,

Like far, sweet songs that come to us,
So soft, so sweet, they are not heard,
So far, so faint, they fill the air,
A fragrance falling anywhere.

And wasting all her summer years
That utter'd only through her tears,
The seasons went, and still she stood
For ever watching down the wood.

Yet in her heart there held a strife
With all this wasting of sweet life,
That none who have not lived and died—
Held up the two hands crucified
Between two ways—can understand.
Men went and came, and still she stood
In silence watching down the wood—
Adown the wood beyond the land,
Her hollow face upon her hand,
Her black, abundant hair all down
About her loose, ungather'd gown.

And what her thought? her life unsaid?
Was it of love? of hate? of him,
The tall, dark Southerner? Her head

Bow'd down.   The day fell dim
Upon her eyes.   She bow'd, she slept.
She waken'd then, and waking wept.

IX.

The black-eyed bushy squirrels ran
Like shadows shatter'd through the boughs;
The gallant robin chirp'd his vows,
The far-off pheasant thrumm'd his fan,
A thousand blackbirds were a-wing
In walnut-top, and it was Spring.

Old Morgan left his cabin door,
And one sat watching as of yore;
But why turn'd Morgan's face as white
As his white beard?   A bird aflight,
A squirrel peering through the trees,
Saw some one silent steal away
Like darkness from the face of day,
Saw two black eyes look back, and these
Saw her hand beckon through the trees.

Ay! they have come, the sun-brown'd men,
To beard old Morgan in his den.

It matters little who they are,
These silent men from isles afar;
And truly no one cares or knows
What be their merit or demand;
It is enough for this rude land—
At least, it is enough for those,
The loud of tongue and rude of hand—
To know that they are Morgan's foes.

Proud Morgan!   More than tongue can tell
He loved that woman watching there,
That stood in her dark stream of hair,
That stood and dream'd as in a spell,
And look'd so fix'd and far away.
And who, that loveth woman well,
Is wholly bad? be who he may.

Ay! we have seen these Southern men,
These sun-brown'd men from island shore,
In this same land, and long before.
They do not seem so lithe as then,
They do not look so tall, and they
Seem not so many as of old.
But that same resolute and bold
Expression of unbridled will,

That even Time must half obey,
Is with them and is of them still.

They do not counsel the decree
Of court or council, where they drew
Their breath, nor law nor order knew,
Save but the strong hand of the strong;
Where each stood up, avenged his wrong,
Or sought his death all silently.
They watch along the wave and wood,
They heed, but haste not.   Their estate,
Whate'er it be, can bide and wait,
Be it open ill or hidden good.
No law for them!   For they have stood
With steel, and writ their rights in blood;
And now, whatever 'tis they seek,
Whatever be their dark demand,
Why, they will make it, hand to hand,
Take time and patience: Greek to Greek.

X.

Like blown and snowy wintry pine,
Old Morgan stoop'd his head and pass'd
Within his cabin door.   He cast

A great arm out to men, made sign,
Then turn'd to Ina; stood beside
A time, then turn'd and strode the floor,
Stopp'd short, breathed sharp, threw wide the
    door,
Then gazed beyond the murky tide,
Toward where the forky peaks divide.

He took his beard in his right hand,
Then slowly shook his grizzled head
And trembled, but no word he said.
His thought was something more than pain;
Upon the seas, upon the land
·He knew he should not rest again.

He turn'd to her; but then once more
Quick turn'd, and through the oaken door
He sudden pointed to the west.
His eye resumed its old command,
The conversation of his hand
It was enough: she knew the rest.

He turn'd, he stoop'd, and smooth'd her hair,
As if to smooth away the care
From his great heart, with his left hand.

His right hand hitch'd the pistol round
That dangled at his belt.   The sound
Of steel to him was melody
More sweet than any song of sea.
He touch'd his pistol, push'd his lips,
Then tapp'd it with his finger-tips,
And toy'd with it as harper's hand
Seeks out the chords when he is sad
And purposeless.   At last he had
Resolve.   In haste he touch'd her hair,
Made sign she should arise—prepare
For some long journey, then again
He look'd awest toward the plain:
Toward the land of dreams and space,

The land of silences, the land
Of shoreless deserts sown with sand,
Where Desolation's dwelling is:
The land where, wondering, you say,
What dried-up shoreless sea is this?
Where, wandering, from day to day
You say, To-morrow sure we come
To rest in some cool resting-place,
And yet you journey on through space
While seasons pass, and are struck dumb
With marvel at the distances.

Yea, he would go.   Go utterly
Away, and from all living kind;
Pierce through the distances, and find
New lands.   He had outlived his race.
He stood like some eternal tree
That tops remote Yosemite,
And cannot fall.   He turn'd his face
Again and contemplated space.

And then he raised his hand to vex
His beard, stood still, and there fell down
Great drops from some unfrequent spring,
And streak'd his chanell'd cheeks sun-brown,
And ran uncheck'd, as one who recks
Nor joy, nor tears, nor anything.

And then, his broad breast heaving deep,
Like some dark sea in troubled sleep,
Blown round with groaning ships and wrecks,
He sudden roused himself, and stood
With all the strength of his stern mood,
Then call'd his men, and bade them go
And bring black steeds with banner'd necks,
And strong like burly buffalo.

XI.

The mighty, stolid, still, black men
Their black-maned horses silent drew
Through solemn wood.   One midnight when
The curl'd moon tipp'd her horn, and threw
A black oak's shadow slant across
A low mound hid in leaves and moss,
Old Morgan cautious came and drew
From out the ground, as from a grave,
Great bags all copper-bound and old,
And fill'd, men say, with pirates' gold.

And then they, silent as a dream,
In long black shadow cross'd the stream.
What strength! what strife! what rude unrest!
What shocks! what half-shaped armies met!
A mighty nation moving west,
With all its steely sinews set
Against the living forests.   Hear
The shouts, the shots of pioneer,
The rended forests, rolling wheels,
As if some half-check'd army reels,

Recoils, redoubles, comes again,
Loud sounding like a hurricane.

O bearded, stalwart, westmost men,
So tower-like, so Gothic built!
A kingdom won without the guilt
Of studied battle, that hath been
Your blood's inheritance....Your heirs
Know not your tombs.   The great plough-
      shares
Cleave softly through the mellow loam
Where you have made eternal home,
And set no sign.   Your epitaphs
Are writ in furrows.   Beauty laughs
While through the green ways wandering
Beside her love, slow gathering
White starry-hearted May-time blooms
Above your lowly levell'd tombs;
And then below the spotted sky
She stops, she leans, she wonders why
The ground is heaved and broken so,
And why the grasses darker grow
And droop and trail like wounded wing.

Yea, Time, the grand old harvester,
Has gather'd you from wood and plain.

We call to you again, again;
The rush and rumble of the car
Comes back in answer.   Deep and wide
The wheels of progress have passed on;
The silent pioneer is gone.
His ghost is moving down the trees,
And now we push the memories
Of bluff, bold men who dared and died
In foremost battle, quite aside.

XII.

And all was life at morn, but one,
The tall old sea-king, grim and grey,
Look'd back to where his cabins lay,
And seem'd to hesitate.   He rose.
At last, as from his dream's repose,
From rest that counterfeited rest,
And set his blown beard to the west;
And rode against the setting sun,
Along the levels vast and dun.

His steeds were steady, strong, and fleet,
The best in all the wide west land,
Their manes were in the air, their feet

Seem'd scarce to touch the flying sand.
   They rode like men gone mad, they **fled,**
All day and many days they **ran,**
And in the rear a grey old **man**
Kept watch, and ever turn'd his head
Half eager and half angry, back
Along their dusty desert track.

   And one look'd back, but no man **spoke,**
They rode, they swallowed up the plain;
The sun sank low, he look'd again,
With lifted hand and shaded eyes.
Then far arear he saw uprise,
As if from giant's stride or stoke,
Dun dust, like puffs of battle-smoke.

   He turn'd, his left hand clutch'd the rein,
He struck hard west his high right hand,
His arms were like the limbs of oak;
They knew too well the man's command,
They mounted, plunged ahead again,
And one look'd back, but no man spoke.

   They climb'd the rock-built breasts of **earth,**
The Titan-fronted, blowy steeps

That cradled Time. Where freedom keeps
Her flag of white blown stars unfurl'd,
They turn'd about, they saw the birth
Of sudden dawn upon the world;
Again they gazed; they saw the face
Of God, and named it boundless space.

And they descended and did roam
Through levell'd distances set around
By room. They saw the Silences
Move by and beckon; saw the forms,
The very beards, of burly storms,
And heard them talk like sounding seas.
On unnamed heights, bleak-blown and brown,
And torn like battlements of Mars,
They saw the darknesses come down,
Like curtains loosen'd from the dome
Of God's cathedral, built of stars.

They pitch'd the tent where rivers run
All foaming to the west, and rush
As if to drown the falling sun.
They saw the snowy mountains roll'd,
And heaved along the nameless lands
Like mighty billows; saw the gold

Of awful sunsets; felt the hush
Of heaven when the day sat down,
And drew about his mantle brown,
And hid his face in dusky hands.

The long and lonesome nights! the tent
That nestled soft in sweep of grass,
The hills against the firmament
Where scarce the moving moon could pass;
The cautious camp, the smother'd light,
The silent sentinel at night!

The wild beasts howling from the hill;
The savage prowling swift and still,
And bended as a bow is bent.
Tne arrow sent; the arrow spent
And buried in its bloody place,
The dead man lying on his face!

The clouds of dust, their cloud by day;
Their pillar of unfailing fire
The far North Star. And high, and higher—
They climb'd so high it seemed eftsoon
That they must face the falling moon,
That like some flame-lit ruin lay
Thrown down before their weary way.

They learn'd to read the sign of storms,
The moon's wide circles, sunset bars,
And storm-provoking blood and flame;
And, like the Chaldean shepherds, came
At night to name the moving stars.
In heaven's face they pictured forms
Of beasts, of fishes of the sea.
They watch'd the Great Bear wearily
Rise up and drag his clinking chain
Of stars around the starry main.

XIII.

And why did these same sun-burnt men
Let Morgan gain the plain, and then
Pursue him ever where he fled?
Mostlike they sought his gold alone,
And fear'd to make their quarrel known
Lest it should keep its secret bed;
Mostlike they thought to best prevail
And conquer with united hands
Alone upon the lonesome sands;
Mostlike they had as much to dread;
Mostlike—but I must tell my tale.

And still old Morgan sought the west;
The sea, the utmost sea, and rest.
He climb'd, descended, climb'd again,
Until he stood at last as lone,
As solitary and unknown,
As some lost ship upon the main.

O there was grandeur in his air,
An old-time splendor in his eye,
When he had climb'd at last the high
And rock-built bastions of the plain,
And thrown a-back his blown white hair,
And halting turn'd to look again.

And long, from out his lofty place,
He look'd far down the fading plain
For his pursuers, but in vain.
Yea, he was glad. Across his face
A careless smile was seen to play,
The first for many a stormy day.

He turn'd to Ina, dark, yet fair
As some sad twilight; touch'd her hair,
Stoop'd low, and kiss'd her silently,
Then silent held her to his breast.

Then waved command to his black men,
Look'd east, then mounted slow, and then
Led leisurely against the west.

And why should he who dared to die,
Who more than once with hissing breath
Had set his teeth and pray'd for death,
Have fled these men, or wherefore fly
Before them now? why not defy?

His midnight men were strong and true,
And not unused to strife, and knew
The masonry of steel right well,
And all its signs that lead to hell.

It might have been his youth had wrought
Some wrongs his years would now repair,
That made him fly and still forbear;
It might have been he only sought
To lead them to some fatal snare,
And let them die by piecemeal there.

I trow it was not shame or fear
Of any man or any thing
That death in any shape might bring,

It might have been some lofty sense
Of his own truth and innocence,
And virtues lofty and severe—
Nay, nay! what need of reasons here?

They climb'd to fringe of tossing trees
That bound a mountain's brow like bay,
And through the fragrant boughs a breeze
Blew salt-flood freshness.   Far away,
From mountain brow to desert base
Lay chaos, space, unbounded space,
In one vast belt of purple bound.
The black men cried, "The sea!" They bow'd
Black, woolly heads in hard black hands.
They wept for joy.   They laugh'd, and broke
The silence of an age, and spoke
Of rest at last; and, grouped in bands,
They threw their long black arms about
Each other's necks, and laugh'd aloud,
Then wept again with laugh and shout.

Yet Morgan spake no word, but led
His band with oft-averted head
Right through the cooling trees, till he
Stood out upon the lofty brow

And mighty mountain wall.   And now
The men who shouted, "Lo, the sea!"
Rode in the sun; but silently:
Stood in the sun, then look'd below.
They look'd but once, then look'd away,
Then look'd each other in the face.
They could not lift their brows, nor say,
But held their heads, nor spake, for lo!
Nor sea, nor voice of sea, nor breath
Of sea, but only sand and death,
And one eternity of space.

XIV.

Old Morgan eyed his men, look'd back
Against the groves of tamarack.
Then tapp'd his stirrup-foot, and stray'd
His broad left hand along the mane
Of his strong steed, and careless play'd
His fingers through the silken skein.

And then he spurr'd him to her side,
And reach'd his hand and leaning wide,
He smiling push'd her falling hair

Back from her brow, and kiss'd her there.
Yea, touch'd her softly, as if she
Had been some priceless, tender flower;
Yet touch'd her as one taking leave
Of his one love in lofty tower
Before descending to the sea
Of battle on his battle eve.

A distant shout! quick oaths! alarms!
The black men start up suddenly,
Stand in the stirrup, clutch their arms,
And bare bright arms all instantly.
But he, he slowly turns, and he
Looks all his full soul in her face.
He does not shout, he does not say,
But sits serenely in his place
A time, then slowly turns, looks back
Between the trim-bough'd tamarack,
And up the winding mountain way,
To where the long, strong grasses lay.

He raised his glass in his two hands,
Then in his left hand let it fall,
Then seem'd to count his fingers o'er,
Then reach'd his glass, waved cold commands,

Then tapp'd his stirrup as before,
Stood in the stirrup stern and tall,
Then ran his hand along the mane
Half nervous-like, and that was all.

And then he turn'd, and smiled half sad,
Half desperate, then hitch'd his steel;
Then all his stormy presence had,
As if he kept once more his keel
On listless seas where breakers reel.

He toss'd again his iron hand
Above the deep, steep desert space,
Above the burning seas of sand,
And look'd his black men in the face.
They spake not, nor look'd back again,
They struck the heel, they clutch'd the rein,
And down the darkling plunging steep
They dropp'd toward the dried-up deep.

Below! It seem'd a league below,
The black men rode, and she rode well,
Against the gleaming, sheening haze
That shone like some vast sea ablaze—
That seem'd to gleam, to glint, to glow,
As if it mark'd the shores of hell.

Then Morgan stood alone, look'd back
From off the fierce wall where he stood,
And watch'd his dusk approaching foe.
He saw him creep along his track,
Saw him descending from the wood,
And smiled to see how worn and slow.

Then when his foemen hounding came
In pistol-shot of where he stood,
He wound his hand in his steed's mane,
And plunging to the desert plain,
Threw back his white beard like a cloud,
And looking back did shout aloud
Defiance like a stormy flood,
And shouted "Vasques!" called his name,
And dared him to the desert flame.

A cloud of dust far down the steep,
Where scarce a whirling hawk would sweep
That cloud his foes had follow'd fast,
And Morgan like a cloud had pass'd,
Yet pass'd like some proud king of old;
And now dark Vasques could not hold
Control of his one wild desire
To meet old Morgan, in his ire.

And Morgan heard his oath and shout,
And Morgan turn'd his head once more,
And wheel'd his stout steed short about,
Then seem'd to count their numbers o'er.
And then his right hand touch'd his steel,
And then he tapp'd his iron heel,
And seemed to fight with thought.   At last
As if the final die was cast,
And cast as carelessly as one
Would toss a white coin in the sun,
He touched his rein once more, and then
His right hand laid with idle heed
Along the toss'd mane of his steed.

Pursuer and pursued! who knows
The why he left the breezy pine,
The fragrant tamarack and vine,
Red rose and precious yellow rose!
Nay, Vasques held the vantage ground
Above him by the wooded steep,
And right nor left no passage lay,
And there was left him but that way,—
The way through blood, or to the deep
And lonesome deserts far profound,
That knew not sight of man, nor sound.

Hot Vasques stood upon the rim,
High, bold, and fierce with crag and spire.
He saw a far grey eagle swim,
He saw a black hawk wheel, retire,
And shun that desert wide a-wing,
But saw no other living thing.

And then he turn'd and shook his head.
" And shall we turn aside," he said,
" Or dare this hell? " The men stood still
As leaning on his sterner will.
And then he stopp'd and turn'd again,
And held his broad hand to his brow,
And look'd intent and eagerly.
The far white levels of the plain
Flash'd back like billows. Even now
He thought he saw rise up 'mid sea,
'Mid space, 'mid wastes, 'mid nothingness,
A ship becalm'd as in distress.

The dim sign pass'd as suddenly,
And then his eager eyes grew dazed,—
He brought his two hands to his face.
Again he raised his head, and gazed
With flashing eyes and visage fierce

Far out, and resolute to pierce
The far, far, faint receding reach
Of space and touch its farther beach.
He saw but space, unbounded space;
Eternal space and nothingness,

Then all wax'd anger'd as they gazed
Far out upon the shoreless land,
And clench'd their doubled hands and raised
Their long bare arms, but utter'd not.
At last one started from the band,
He raised his arm, push'd back his sleeve,
Push'd bare his arm, strode up and down,
With hat push'd back. Then flush'd and hot
He shot sharp oaths like cannon shot.

Then Vasques was resolved, his form
Seem'd like a pine blown rampt with storm,
He mounted, clutch'd his reins, and then
Turn'd sharp and savage to his men;
And silent then led down the way
To night that knows not night or day,

xv.

How broken plunged the steep descent!

How barren!   Desolate, and rent
By earthquake's shock, the land lay dead,
With dust and ashes on its head.

'Twas as some old world overthrown
Where Theseus fought and Sappho dream'd
In æons ere they touch'd this land,
And found their proud souls foot and hand
Bound to the flesh and stung with pain.
An ugly skeleton it seem'd
Of its old self.   The fiery rain
Of red volcanoes here had sown
The death of cities of the plain.
Ay, vanquish'd quite and overthrown,
And torn with thunder-stroke, and strown
With cinders, lo! the dead earth lay
As waiting for the judgment day.
Why, tamer men had turn'd and said,
On seeing this, with start and dread,
And whisper'd each with gather'd breath.
"We come on the confines of death."

They wound below a savage bluff
That lifted, from its sea-mark'd base,
Great walls with characters cut rough

And deep by some long-perish'd race;
And great, strange beasts unnamed, unknown,
Stood hewn and limn'd upon the stone.

A mournful land as land can be
Beneath their feet in ashes lay,
Beside that dread and dried-up sea;
A city older than that grey
And grass-grown tower builded when
Confusion cursed the tongues of men.

Beneath, before, a city lay
That in her majesty had shamed
The wolf-nursed conqueror of old;
Below, before, and far away,
There reach'd the white arm of a bay,
A broad bay shrunk to sand and stone,
Where ships had rode and breakers roll'd
When Babylon was yet unnamed,
And Nimrod's hunting-fields unknown.

Some serpents slid from out the grass
That grew in tufts by shatter'd stone,
Then hid beneath some broken mass
That Time had eaten as a bone

Is eaten by some savage beast;
An everlasting palace feast.

A dull-eyed rattlesnake that lay
All loathsome, yellow-skinn'd, and slept,
Coil'd tight as pine-knot, in the sun,
With flat head through the centre run,
Struck blindly back, then rattling crept
Flat-bellied down the dusty way . . .
'Twas all the dead land had to say.

Two pink-eyed hawks, wide-wing'd and grey,
Scream'd savagely, and, circling high,
And screaming still in mad dismay,
Grew dim and died against the sky . . .
'Twas all the heavens had to say.

The sun rose right above, and fell
As falling molten as they pass'd.
Some low-built junipers at last,
The last that o'er the desert look'd,
Thick-bough'd, and black as shapes of hell,
Where dumb owls sat with bent bills hook'd
Beneath their wings awaiting night,
Rose up, then faded from the sight:

Then not another living thing
Crept on the sand or kept the wing.

White Azteckee! Dead Azteckee!
Vast sepulchre of buried sea!
What dim ghosts hover on thy rim,
What stately-manner'd shadows swim
Along thy gleaming waste of sands
And shoreless limits of dead lands?

Dread Azteckee! Dead Azteckee!
White place of ghosts, give up thy dead:
Give back to Time thy buried hosts!
The new world's tawny Ishmaelite,
The roving tent-born Shoshonee,
Who shuns thy shores as death, at night
Because thou art so white, so dread,
Because thou art so ghostly white,
Has named thy shores " the place of ghosts."

Thy white, uncertain sands are white
With bones of thy unburied dead,
That will not perish from the sight.
They drown, but perish not—ah me!

What dread unsightly sights are spread
Along this lonesome, dried-up sea?

Old, hoar, and dried-up sea! so old!
So strown with wealth, so sown with gold!
Yea, thou art old and hoary white
With time, and ruin of all things;
And on thy lonesome borders night
Sits brooding as with wounded wings.

The winds that toss'd thy waves and blew
Across thy breast the blowing sail,
And cheer'd the hearts of cheering crew
From farther seas, no more prevail.
Thy white-wall'd cities all lie prone.
With but a pyramid, a stone,
Set head and foot in sands to tell
The tired stranger where they fell.

The patient ox that bended low
His neck, and drew slow up and down
Thy thousand freights through rock-built
    town
Is now the free-born buffalo.
No longer of the timid fold,

12

The mountain ram leaps free and bold
His high-built summit, and looks down
From battlements of buried town.

Thine ancient steeds know not the rein;
They lord the land; they come, they go
At will; they laugh at man; they blow
A cloud of black steeds o'er the plain.
Thy monuments lie buried now,
The ashes whiten on thy brow,
The winds, the waves, have drawn away—
The very wild man dreads to stay.

XVI.

Away upon the sandy seas,
The gleaming, burning, boundless plain.
How solemn-like, how still, as when
The mighty minded Genoese
Drew three slim ships and led his men
From land they might not meet again.

The black men rode in front by two,
The fair one follow'd close, and kept

Her face held down as if she wept;
But Morgan kept the rear, and threw
His flowing, swaying beard still back
In watch along their lonesome track.

The weary day fell down to rest,
A star upon his mantled breast,
Ere scarce the sun fell out of space,
And Venus glimmer'd in his place.
Yea, all the stars shone just as fair,
And constellations kept their round,
And look'd from out the great profound,
And march'd, and countermarch'd, and shone
Upon that desolation there—
Why, just the same as if proud man
Strode up and down array'd in gold
And purple as in days of old,
And reckon'd all of his own plan,
Or made at least for man alone.

Yet on push'd Morgan silently,
And straight as strong ship on a sea;
And ever as he rode there lay
To right, to left, and in his way,
Strange objects looming in the dark,
Some like a mast, or ark, or bark.

And things half-hidden in the sand
Lay down before them where they pass'd,—
A broken beam, half-buried mast,
A spar or bar, such as might be
Blown crosswise, tumbled on the strand
Of some sail-crowded stormy sea.

All night by moon, by morning star,
The still, black men still kept their way;
All night till morn, till burning day,
Hard Vasques follow'd fast and far.

The sun is high, the sands are hot
To touch, and all the tawny plain
Sinks white and open as they tread
And trudge, with half-averted head,
As if to swallow them in sand.
They look, as men look back to land
When standing out to stormy sea,
But still keep pace and murmur not;
Keep stern and still as destiny.

It was a sight! A slim dog slid
White-mouth'd and still along the sand,
The pleading picture of distress.

He stopp'd, leap'd up to lick a hand,
A hard, black hand that sudden chid
Him back, and check'd his tenderness.
Then when the black man turn'd his head,
His poor, mute friend had fallen dead.

The very air hung white with heat,
And white, and fair, and far away
A lifted, shining snow-shaft lay
As if to mock their mad retreat.
The white, salt sands beneath their feet
Did make the black men loom as grand,
From out the lifting, heaving heat,
As they rode sternly on and on,
As any bronze men in the land
That sit their statue steeds upon.

The men were silent as men dead.
The sun hung centred overhead,
Nor seem'd to move. It molten hung
Like some great central burner swung
From lofty beams with golden bars
In sacristy set round with stars.

Why, flame could hardly be more hot;
Yet on the mad pursuer came

Across the gleaming, yielding ground,
Right on, as if he fed on flame,
Right on until the mid-day found
The man within a pistol-shot.

He hail'd, but Morgan answer'd not;
He hail'd, then came a feeble shot,
And strangely, in that vastness there,
It seem'd to scarcely fret the air,
But fell down harmless anywhere.

He fiercely hail'd; and then there fell
A horse.   And then a man fell down,
And in the sea-sand seem'd to drown.
Then Vasques cursed, but scarce could tell
The sound of his own voice, and all
In mad confusion seem'd to fall.

Yet on pushed Morgan, silent on,
And as he rode, he lean'd and drew
From his catenas gold, and threw
The bright coins in the glaring sun.
But Vasques did not heed a whit,
He scarcely deign'd to scowl at it.

Again lean'd Morgan. 'He uprose,

And held a high hand to his foes,
And held two goblets up, and one
Did shine as if itself a sun.
Then leaning backward from his place,
He hurl'd them in his foeman's face;
Then drew again, and so kept on,
Till goblets, gold, and all were gone.

Yea, strew'd them out upon the sands
As men upon a frosty morn,
In Mississippi's fertile lands,
Hurl out great yellow ears of corn,
To hungry swine with hurried hands.

Yet still hot Vasques urges on,
With flashing eye and flushing cheek.
What would he have? what does he seek?
He does not heed the gold a whit,
He does not deign to look at it;
But now his gleaming steel is drawn,
And now he leans, would hail again,—
He opes his swollen lips in vain.

But look you! See! A lifted hand,
And Vasques beckons his command.

He cannot speak, he leans, and he
Bends low upon his saddle-bow.
And now his blade drops to his knee,
And now he falters, now comes on,
And now his head is bended low;
And now his rein, his steel, is gone;
Now faint as any child is he,
And now his steed sinks to the knee.

The sun hung molten in mid-space,
Like some great star fix'd in its place.
From out the gleaming spaces rose
A sheen of gossamer and danced,
As Morgan slow and still advanced
Before his far-receding foes.
Right on, and on, the still, black line
Drove straight through gleaming sand and
    shine,
By spar and beam and mast, and stray
And waif of sea and cast-away.

The far peaks faded from their sight,
The mountain walls fell down like night,
And nothing now was to be seen
Except the dim sun hung in sheen

Of fairy garments all blood-red,—
The hell beneath, the hell o'erhead.

A black man tumbled from his steed.
He clutch'd in death the moving sands,
He caught the hot earth in his hands,
He gripp'd it, held it hard and grim....
The great, sad mother did not heed
His hold, but pass'd right on from him.

XVII.

The sun seem'd broken loose at last,
And settled slowly to the west,
Half-hidden as he fell to rest,
Yet, like the flying Parthian, cast
His keenest arrows as he pass'd.

On, on, the black men slowly drew
Their length like some great serpent through
The sands, and left a hollow'd groove:
They march'd, they scarcely seem'd to move.
How patient in their muffled tread!
How like the dead march of the dead!

At last the slow, black line was check'd,
An instant only; now again
It moved, it falter'd now, and now
It settled in its sandy bed,
And steeds stood rooted to the plain.
Then all stood still, and men somehow
Look'd down and with averted head;
Look'd down, nor dared look up, nor reck'd
Of anything, of ill or good,
But bow'd and stricken still they stood.

Like some brave band that dared the fierce
And bristled steel of gather'd host,
These daring men had dared to pierce
This awful vastness, dead and grey.
And now at last brought well at bay
They stood,—but each stood to his post.

Then one dismounted, waved a hand,
'Twas Morgan's stern and still command.
There fell a clank, like loosen'd chain,
And men dismounting loosed the rein.
Then every steed stood loosed and free;
And some stepp'd slow and mute aside,
And some sank to the sands and died;
And some stood still as shadows be.

Old Morgan turn'd and raised his hand.
And laid it level with his eyes,
And look'd far back along the land.
He saw a dark dust still uprise,
Still surely tend to where he lay.
He did not curse, he did not say—
He did not even look surprise.

Nay, he was over-gentle now;
He wiped a time his Titan brow,
Then sought dark Ina in her place,
Put out his arms, put down his face
And look'd in hers.   She reach'd her hands,
She lean'd, she fell upon his breast;
He reach'd his arms around; she lay
As lies a bird in leafy nest.
And he look'd out across the sands,
Then bearing her, he strode away.

Some black men settled down to rest,
But none made murmur or request.
The dead were dead, and that were best;
The living leaning follow'd him,
In huddled heaps, all hush'd and grim.

The day through high mid-heaven rode
Across the sky, the dim, red day;
And on, the warlike day-god strode
With shoulder'd shield away, away.

The savage, warlike day bent low,
As reapers bend in gathering grain,
As archer bending bends yew bow,
And flush'd and fretted as in pain.

Then down his shoulder slid his shield,
So huge, so awful, so blood-red
And batter'd as from battle-field:
It settled, sunk to his left hand,
Sunk down and down, it touch'd the sand;
Then day along the land lay dead,
Without one candle at his head.

And now the moon wheel'd white and vast,
A round, unbroken, marbled moon,
And touch'd the far, bright buttes of snow,
Then climb'd their shoulders over soon;
And there she seem'd to sit at last,
To hang, to hover there, to grow,
Grow vaster than vast peaks of snow.

She sat the battlements of time;
She shone in mail of frost and rime,
A time, and then rose up and stood
In heaven in sad widowhood.

The faded moon fell wearily,
And then the sun right suddenly
Rose up full arm'd, and rushing came
Across the land like flood of flame.

And now it look'd as hills uprose,
High push'd against the arching skies,
As if to meet the sudden sun—
Rose sharp from out the sultry dun,
And seem'd to hold the free repose
Of lands where flow'ry summits rise,
In unfenced fields of Paradise.

The black men look'd up from the sands
Against the dim, uncertain skies,
As men that disbelieved their eyes,
And would have laugh'd; they wept instead,
With shoulders heaved, with bowing head
Hid down between the two black hands.

They stood and gazed. Lo! like the call

Of spring-time promises, the trees
Lean'd from their lifted mountain wall,
And stood clear cut against the skies,
As if they grew in pistol-shot.
Yet all the mountains answer'd not,
And yet there came no cooling breeze,
Nor soothing sense of windy trees.

At last old Morgan, looking through
His shaded fingers, let them go,
And let his load fall down as dead.
He groan'd, he clutch'd his beard of snow
As was his wont, then bowing low,
Took up his life, and moaning said,
"Lord Christ! 'tis the mirage, and we
Stand blinded in a burning sea."

XVIII.

Again they move, but where or how
It recks them little, nothing now.
Yet Morgan leads them as before,
But totters now; he bends, and he
Is like a broken ship a-sea,—

A ship that knows not any shore,
And knows it shall not anchor more.

Some leaning shadows crooning crept
Through desolation, crown'd in dust.
And had the mad pursuer kept
His path, and cherish'd his pursuit?
There lay no choice.   Advance, he must:
Advance, and eat his ashen fruit.

Yet on and on old Morgan led.
His black men totter'd to and fro,
A leaning, huddled heap of woe;
Then one fell down, then two fell dead;
Yet not one moaning word was said.
They made no sign, they said no word,
Nor lifted once black, helpless hands;
And all the time no sound was heard
Save but the dull, dead, muffled tread
Of shuffled feet in shining sands.

Again the still moon rose and stood
Above the dim, dark belt of wood,
Above the buttes, above the snow,
And bent a sad, sweet face below.

She reach'd along the level plain
Her long, white fingers.   Then again
She reach'd, she touch'd the snowy sands.
Then reach'd far out until she touch'd
A heap that lay with doubled hands,
Reach'd from its sable self, and clutch'd
With death.   O tenderly
That black, that dead and hollow face
Was kiss'd at midnight....What if I say
The long, white moonbeams reaching there,
Caressing idle hands of clay,
And resting on the wrinkled hair
And great lips push'd in silent pout,
Were God's own fingers reaching out
From heaven to that lonesome place?

XIX.

By waif and stray and cast-away,
Such as are seen in seas withdrawn,
Old Morgan led in silence on,
And sometimes lifting up his head,
To guide his footsteps as he led,
He deem'd he saw a great ship lay

Her keel along the sea-wash'd sand, ·
As with her captain's old command.

  The stars were seal'd; and then a haze
Of gossamer fill'd all the west,
So like in Indian summer days,
And veil'd all things.   And then the moon
Grew pale, and faint, and far.   She died,
And now nor star nor any sign
Fell out of heaven.   Oversoon
Some black men fell.   Then at their side
Some one sat down to watch, to rest....
To rest, to watch, or what you will,
The man sits resting, watching still.

XX.

  The day glared through the eastern rim
Of rocky peaks, as prison bars
With light as dim as distant stars.
The sultry sunbeams filter'd down
Through misty phantoms weird and dim,
Through shifting shapes bat-wing'd and ·
    brown.

Like some vast ruin wrapp'd in flame
The sun fell down before them now.
Behind them wheel'd white peaks of snow,
As they proceeded. Grey and grim ,
And awful objects went and came
Before them then. They pierced at last
The desert's middle depths, and lo!
There loom'd from out the desert vast
A lonely ship, well-built and trim,
And perfect all in hull and mast.

No storm had stain'd it any whit,
No seasons set their teeth in it.
Her masts were white as ghosts, and tall;
Her decks were as of yesterday.
The rains, the elements, and all
The moving things that bring decay
By fair green lands or fairer seas,
Had touch'd not here for centuries.
Lo! date had lost all reckoning,
And Time had long forgotten all
In this lost land, and no new thing
Or old could anywise befall,
For Time went by the other way.

What dreams of gold or conquest drew

The oak-built sea-king to these seas,
Ere Earth, old Earth, unsatisfied,
Rose up and shook man in disgust
From off her wearied breast, and threw
His high-built cities down, and dried
These measured ship-sown seas to dust?
Who trod these decks? What captain knew
The straits that led to lands like these?

Blew south-sea breeze or north-sea breeze?
What spiced-winds whistled through this sail?
What banners stream'd above these seas?
And what strange seaman answer'd back
To other sea-king's beck and hail,
That blew across his foamy track?

Sought Jason here the golden fleece?
Came Trojan ship or ships of Greece?
Came decks dark-mann'd from sultry Ind,
Woo'd here by spacious wooing wind?
So like a grand, sweet woman, when
A great love moves her soul to men?

Came here strong ships of Solomon
In quest of Ophir by Cathay? . . .

Sit down and dream of seas withdrawn,
And every sea-breath drawn away.
Sit down, sit down! What is the good
That we go on still fashioning
Great iron ships or walls of wood,
High masts of oak, or anything?

Lo! all things moving must go by.
The sea lies dead. Behold, this land
Sits desolate in dust beside
His snow-white, seamless shroud of sand;
The very clouds have wept and died,
And only God is in the sky.

XXI.

The sands lay heaved, as heaved by waves,
As fashion'd in a thousand graves:
And wrecks of storm blown here and there,
And dead men scatter'd everywhere;
And strangely clad they seem'd to be
Just as they sank in that old sea.

The mermaid with her splendid hair
Had clung about a wreck's beam there;

And sung her song of sweet despair,
The time she saw the seas withdrawn
And all her home and glory gone:
Had sung her melancholy dirge
Above the last receding surge,
And, looking down the rippled tide,
Had sung, and with her song had died.

The monsters of the sea lay bound
In strange contortions. Coil'd around
A mast half heaved above the sand,
The great sea-serpent's folds were found,
As solid as ship's iron band.
And basking in the burning sun
There rose the great whale's skeleton.

A thousand sea things stretch'd across
Their weary and bewilder'd way:
Great unnamed monsters wrinkled lay
With sunken eyes and shrunken form.
The strong sea-horse that rode the storm
With mane as light and white as floss,
Lay tangled in his mane of moss.

And anchor, hull, and cast-away,
And all things that the miser deep

Doth in his darkling locker keep,
To right and left around them lay.
Yea, golden coin and golden cup,
And golden cruse, and golden plate,
And all that great seas swallow up,
Right in their dreadful pathway lay.
The hoary sea made white with time,
And wrinkled cross with many a crime,
With all his treasured thefts was there,
His sins, his very soul laid bare,
As if it were the Judgment Day.

XXII.

And now the tawny night fell soon,
And there was neither star nor moon;
And yet it seem'd it was not night.
There fell a phosphorescent light,
There rose from white sands and dead men
A soft light, white and strange as when
The Spirit of Jehovah moved
Upon the water's conscious face,
And made it His abiding-place.

Remote, around the lonesome ship,

Old Morgan moved, but knew it not,
For neither star nor moon fell down . . . .
I trow that was a lonesome spot
He found, where boat and ship did dip
In sands like some half-sunken town.

At last before the leader lay
A form that in the night did seem
A slain Goliath.   As in a dream,
He drew aside in his slow pace,
And look'd. He saw a sable face!
A friend that fell that very day,
Thrown straight across his wearied way!

He falter'd now.   His iron heart,
That never yet refused its part,
Began to fail him; and his strength
Shook at his knees, as shakes the wind
A shatter'd ship. His scatter'd mind
Ranged up and down the land. At length
He turn'd, as ships turn, tempest toss'd,
For now he knew that he was lost!
He sought in vain the moon, the stars,
In vain the battle-star of Mars.

Again he moved.   And now again
He paused, he peer'd along the plain,
Another form before him lay.
He stood, and statue-white he stood,
He trembled like a stormy wood,—
It was a foeman brawn and grey.

He lifted up his head again,
Again he search'd the great profound
For moon, for star, but sought in vain.
He kept his circle round and round
The great ship lifting from the sand,
And pointing heavenward like a hand.

And still he crept along the plain,
Yet where his foeman dead again
Lay in his way he moved around,
And soft as if on sacred ground,
And did not touch him anywhere.
It might have been he had a dread,
In his half-crazed and fever'd brain,
His mortal foe might wake again
If he should dare to touch him there.

He circled round the lonesome ship
Like some wild beast within a wall,

That keeps his paces round and round.
The very stillness had a sound;
He saw strange somethings rise and dip;
He felt the weirdness like a pall
Come down and cover him. It seem'd
To take a form, take many forms,
To talk to him, to reach out arms;
Yet on he kept, and silent kept,
And as he led he lean'd and slept,
And as he slept he talk'd and dream'd.

Then shadows follow'd, stopp'd, and stood
Bewilder'd, wander'd back again,
Came on and then fell to the sand,
And sinking died. Then other men
Did wag their woolly heads and laugh,
Then bend their necks and seem to quaff
Of cooling waves that careless flow
Where woods and long, strong grasses grow.

Yet on wound Morgan, leaning low,
With her upon his breast, and slow
As hand upon a dial plate.
He did not turn his course or quail,
He did not falter, did not fail,
Turn right or left or hesitate.

Some far-off sounds had lost their way,
And seem'd to call to him and pray
For help, as if they were affright,
It was not day, it seem'd not night,
But that dim land that lies between
The mournful, faithful face of night,
And loud and gold-bedazzled day;
A night that was not felt but seen.

There seem'd not then the ghost of sound,
He stepp'd as soft as step the dead; .
Yet on he led in solemn tread,
Bewilder'd, blinded, round and round,
About the great black ship that rose
Tall-masted as that ship that blows
Her ghost below lost Panama,—
The tallest mast man ever saw.

Two leaning shadows follow'd him:
Their eyes were red, their teeth shone white,
Their limbs did lift as shadows swim.
Then one went left and one went right,
And in the night pass'd out of night;
Pass'd through the portals black, unknown,
And Morgan totter'd on alone.

And why he still survived the rest,
Why still he had the strength to stir,
Why still he stood like gnarled oak
That buffets storm and tempest stroke,
One cannot say, save but for her,
That helpless being on his breast.

She did not speak, she did not stir;
In rippled currents over her,
Her black, abundant hair pour'd down
Like mantle or some sable gown.
That sad, sweet dreamer; she who knew
Not anything of earth at all,
Nor cared to know its bane or bliss;
That dove that did not touch the land,
That knew, yet did not understand.
And this may be because she drew
Her all of life right from the hand
Of God, and did not choose to learn
The things that make up earth's concern.

Ah! there be souls none understand;
Like clouds, they cannot touch the land.
Unanchor'd ships, they blow and blow,
Sail to and fro, and then go down

In unknown seas that none shall know,
Without one ripple of renown.

Call these not fools; the test of worth
Is not the hold you have of earth.
Ay, there be gentlest souls sea-blown
That know not any harbor known.
Now it may be the reason is,
They touch on fairer shores than this.

At last he touch'd a fallen group,
Dead fellows tumbled in the sands,
Dead foemen, gather'd to the dead.
And eager now the man did stoop,
Lay down his load and reach his hands,
And stretch his form and look steadfast
And frightful, and as one aghast.
He lean'd, and then he raised his head,
And look'd for Vasques, but in vain
He peer'd along the deadly plain.

Lo! from the night another face,
The last that follow'd through the deep,
Comes on, falls dead within a pace.
Yet Vasques still survives! But where?

His last bold follower lies there,
Thrown straight across old Morgan's track,
As if to check him, bid him back.
He stands, he does not dare to stir,
He watches by his bride asleep,
He fears for her: but only her.
The man who ever mock'd at death,
He hardly dares to draw his breath.

XXIII.

Beyond, and still as black despair,
A man rose up, stood dark and tall,
Stretch'd out his neck, reach'd forth, let fall
Dark oaths, and Death stood waiting there.

He drew his blade, came straight as death
For Morgan's last man, most endear'd.
I think no man there drew a breath,
I know that no man quail'd or fear'd.

The tawny dead man stretch'd between,
And Vasques set his foot thereon.
The stars were seal'd, the moon was gone,

The very darkness cast a shade.
The scene was rather heard than seen,
The rattle of a single blade....

A right foot rested on the dead,
A black hand reach'd and clutch'd a beard,
Then neither pray'd, nor dream'd of hope.
A fierce face reach'd, a black face peer'd....
No bat went whirling overhead,
No star fell out of Ethiope.

The dead man lay between them there,
The two men glared as tigers glare,—
The black man held him by the beard.
He wound his hand, he held him fast,
And tighter held, as if he fear'd
The man might 'scape him at the last.
Whiles Morgan did not speak or stir,
But stood in silent watch by her.

Not long....A light blade lifted, thrust,
A blade that leapt and swept about,
So wizard-like, like wand in spell,
So like a serpent's tongue thrust out....
Thrust twice, thrust thrice, thrust as he fell,
Thrust through until it touched the dust.

Yet ever as he thrust and smote,
A black hand like an iron band
Did tighten round a gasping throat.
He fell, but did not loose his hand;
The two fell dead upon the sand.

Lo! up and from the fallen forms
Two ghosts came forth like clouds of storms;
Two grey ghosts stood, then looking back,
With hands all empty, and hands clutch'd,
Strode on in silence.   Then they touch'd,
Along the lonesome, chartless track,
Where dim Plutonian darkness fell,
Then touch'd the outer rim of hell;
And looking back their great despair
Sat sadly down, as resting there.

XXIV.

As if there was a strength in death
The battle seem'd to nerve the man
To superhuman strength.   He rose,
Held up his head, began to scan
The heavens and to take his breath

Right strong and lustily.   He now
Resumed his load, and with his eye
Fix'd on a star that filter'd through
The farther west, push'd bare his brow,
And kept his course with head held high,
As if he strode his deck and drew
His keel below some lifted light
That watch'd the rocky reef at night.

How lone he was, how patient she
Upon that lonesome sandy sea!
It were a sad, unpleasant sight
To follow them through all the night,
Until the time they lifted hand,
And touch'd at last a water'd land.

There turkeys walk'd the tangled grass,
And scarcely turn'd to let them pass.
There was no sign of man, nor sign
Of savage beast.   'Twas so divine,
It seem'd as if the bended skies
Were rounded for this Paradise.

The large-eyed antelope came down
From off their windy hills, and blew

Their whistles as they wander'd through
The open groves of water'd wood;
Then came as light as if on wing,
And reached their noses wet and brown,
And stamp'd their little feet and stood
Close up before them wondering.

What if this were the Eden true,
They found in far heart of the new
And unnamed westmost world I sing,
Where date and history had birth,
And man first 'gan his wandering
To go the girdles of the earth!

It lies a little isle mid land,
An island in a sea of sand;
With reedy waters and the balm
Of an eternal summer air;
Some blowy pines toss tall and fair;
And there are grasses long and strong,
And tropic fruits that never fail:
The Manzinetta pulp, the palm,
The prickly pear, with all the song
Of summer birds.   And there the quail

14

Makes nest, and you may hear her call
All day from out the chaparral.

A land where white man never trod,
And Morgan seems some demi-god,
That haunts the red man's spirit-land.
A land where never red man's hand
Is lifted up in strife at all,
But holds it sacred unto those
Who bravely fell before their foes,
And rarely dares its desert wall.

Here breaks nor sound of strife nor sign;
Rare times a red man comes this way,
Alone, and battle-scarr'd and grey,
And then he bends devout before
The maid who keeps the cabin-door,
And deems her something all divine.

Within the island's heart 'tis said,
Tall trees are bending down with bread,
And that a fountain pure as Truth,
And deep and mossy-bound and fair,
Is bubbling from the forest there,—
Perchance the fabled fount of youth!

An isle where skies are ever fair,
Where men keep never date nor day,
Where Time has thrown his glass away.

This isle is all their own.   No more
The flight by day, the watch by night.
Dark Ina twines about the door
The scarlet blooms, the blossoms white
And winds red berries in her hair,
And never knows the name of care.

She has a thousand birds; they blow
In rainbow clouds, in clouds of snow;
The birds take berries from her hand;
They come and go at her command.
She has a thousand pretty birds,
That sing her summer songs all day;
Small, black-hoof'd antelope in herds,
And squirrels bushy-tail'd and grey,
With round and sparkling eyes of pink,
And cunning-faced as you can think.

She has a thousand busy birds;
And is she happy in her isle,

With all her feather'd friends and herds?
For when has Morgan seen her smile?

She has a thousand cunning birds,
They would build nestings in her hair,
She has brown antelope in herds;
She never knows the name of care;
Why, then, is she not happy there?
All patiently she bears her part;
She has a thousand birdlings there,
These birds they would build in her hair;
But not one bird builds in her heart.

She has a thousand birds; yet she
Would give ten thousand cheerfully,
All bright of plume and pure of tongue,
And sweet as ever trilled or sung,
For one small flutter'd bird to come
And build within her heart, though dumb.

She has a thousand birds; yet one
Is lost, and, lo! she is undone.
She sighs sometimes. She looks away,
And yet she does not weep or say.

NOTE.—This story, if story it is, I learned from the lips of Mountain Joe, of Utah. The desert is certainly the bed of a dried-up sea, of which Great Salt Lake is a northern remnant. Indeed, as you look across Salt Lake to the west, you can see on the mountain side, fifty feet above the present water level, a well-defined sea shore.

The Ship in the Desert is counted a veritable fact by many good men. I have been on the borders of this desert, but further than some old bits of battered copper, I am bound to say that I found no evidence of its existence. But the late Colonel Evans, of California, a man much respected, and author of a work on this subject, told me that by the aid of a powerful fieldglass, and under a peculiarly favorable light, he had seen the ship. My honest opinion is that it was but a mirage.

L O! here sit we by the sun-down seas
    And the white Sierras. The sweet sea-breeze
Is about us here; and a sky so fair
  Is bending above, so cloudless, blue,
    That you gaze and you gaze and you dream, and you
See God and the portals of heaven there.

SHAKE hands! kiss hands in haste to the
        sea,
Where the sun comes in, and mount with me
The matchless steed of the strong New World,
As he champs and chafes with a strength
        untold,—
And away to the West, where the waves are
        curl'd,
As they kiss white palms to the capes of gold!

A girth of brass and a breast of steel,
A breath of fire and a flaming mane,
An iron hoof and a steel-clad heel,
A Mexican bit and a massive chain

Well tried and wrought in an iron rein;
And away! away! with a shout and yell
They had stricken a legion of old with fear,
They had started the dead from the graves
    whilere,
And startled the damn'd in hell as well.

Stand up! stand out! where the wind comes in,
And the wealth of the seas pours over you,
As its health floods up to the face like wine,
And a breath blows up from the Delaware
And the Susquehanna. We feel the might
Of armies in us; the blood leaps through
The frame with a fresh and a keen delight
As the Alleghanies have kiss'd the hair,
With a kiss blown far through the rush and din,
By the chestnut burs and through boughs of
    pine.

O seas in a land! O lakes of mine!
By the love I bear and the songs I bring
Be glad with me! lift your waves and sing
A song in the reeds that surround your isles!—
A song of joy for this sun that smiles,
For this land I love and this age and sign;

For the peace that is and the perils pass'd;
For the hope that is and the rest at last! ·

O heart of the world's heart! West! my West!
Look up! look out! There are fields of kine,
There are clover-fields that are red as wine;
And a world of kine in the fields take rest,
As they ruminate in the shade of trees
That are white with blossoms or brown with bees.

There are emerald seas of corn and cane;
There are isles of oak on the harvest plain,
Where brown men bend to the bending grain;
There are temples of God and towns new-born,
And beautiful homes of beautiful brides;
And the hearts of oak and the hands of horn
Have fashion'd them all and a world besides. . .

A rush of rivers and a brush of trees,
A breath blown far from the Mexican seas,
And over the great heart-vein of earth!
. . . By the South-Sun-land of the Cherokee,
By the scalp-lock-lodge of the tall Pawnee,
And up the La Platte. What a weary dearth
Of the homes of men! What a wild delight

Of space! Of room! What a sense of seas,
Where the seas are not! What a salt-like
    breeze!
What dust and taste of quick alkali!
. . . Then hills! green, brown, then black like
    night,
All fierce and defiant against the sky!

  At last! at last! O steed new-born,
Born strong of the will of the strong New World,
We shoot to the summit, with the shafts of morn,
On the mount of Thunder, where clouds are
    curl'd,
Below in a splendor of the sun-clad seas.
A kiss of welcome on the warm west breeze
Blows up with a smell of the fragrant pine,
And a faint, sweet fragrance from the far-off seas
Comes in through the gates of the great South
    Pass
And thrills the soul like a flow of wine.
The hare leaps low in the storm-bent grass,
The mountain ram from his cliffs looks back,
The brown deer hies to the tamarack;
And afar to the South with a sound of the main,
Roll buffalo herds to the limitless plain . . . .

On, on, o'er the summit; and onward again,
And down like the sea-dove the billow en-
    shrouds,
And down like the swallow that dips to the sea,
We dart and we dash and we quiver and we
Are blowing to heaven white billows of clouds.

Thou "City of Saints!" O antique men,
And men of the Desert as the men of old!
Stand up! be glad! When the truths are told,
When Time has utter'd his truths and when
His hand has lifted the things to fame
From the mass of things to be known no more,
A monument set in the desert sand,
A pyramid rear'd on an inland shore,
And their architects, shall have place and name.

The Humboldt desert and the alkaline land,
And the seas of sage and of arid sand
That stretch away till the strain'd eye carries
The soul where the infinite spaces fill,
Are far in the rear, and the fierce Sierras
Are under our feet, and the heart beats high
And the blood comes quick; but the lips are
    still

With awe and wonder, and all the will
Is bow'd with a grandeur that frets the sky.

A flash of lakes through the fragrant trees,
A song of birds and a sound of bees
Above in the boughs of the sugar-pine.
The pick-axe stroke in the placer mine,
The boom of blasts in the gold-ribbed hills,
The grizzly's growl in the gorge below
Are dying away, and the sound of rills
From the far-off shimmering crest of snow,
The laurel green and the ivied oak,
A yellow stream and a cabin's smoke,
The brown bent hills and the shepherd's call,
The hills of vine and of fruits, and all
The sweets of Eden are here, and we
Look out and afar to a limitless sea.

We have lived an age in a half-moon-wane!
We have seen a world! We have chased the sun
From sea to sea; but the task is done.
We here descend to the great white main,—
To the King of Seas, with the temples bare
And a tropic breath on the brow and hair.

We are hush'd with wonder, we stand apart,
We stand in silence; the heaving heart
Fills full of heaven, and then the knees
Go down in worship on the golden sands.
With faces seaward, and with folded hands
We gaze on the beautiful Balboa seas.

AN INDIAN SUMMER.

*T*HE *world it is wide; men go their ways;*
    But love he is wise, and of all the hours,
And of all the beautiful sun-born days,
  He sips their sweets as the bees sip flowers.

T HE sunlight lay in gather'd sheaves
    Along the ground, the golden leaves
Possess'd the land and lay in bars
Above the lifted lawn of green
Beneath the feet, or fell, as stars
Fall, slantwise, shimmering and still
Upon the plain, upon the hill,
And heaving hill and plain between.

  Some steeds in panoply were seen,
Strong, martial trained, with manes in air,
And tassell'd reins and mountings rare;
Some silent people here and there,
That gather'd leaves with listless will,
Or moved adown the dappled green,

Or look'd away with idle gaze
Against the gold and purple haze.
You might have heard red leaflets fall,
The pheasant on the farther hill,
A single, lonely, locust trill,
Or sliding sable cricket call
From out the grass, but that was all.

A wanderer of many lands
Was I, a weary Ishmaelite,
That knew the sign of lifted hands;
Had seen the Crescent-mosques, had seen
The Druid oaks of Aberdeen—
Recross'd the hilly seas, and saw
The sable pines of Mackinaw,
And lakes that lifted cold and white.

I saw the sweet Miami, saw
The swift Ohio bent and roll'd
Between his gleaming walls of gold,
The Wabash banks of gray pawpaw,
The Mississippi's ash; at morn
Of autumn, when the oak is red,
Saw slanting pyramids of corn,
The level fields of spotted swine,

The crooked lanes of lowing kine,
And in the burning bushes saw
The face of God, with bended head.

But when I saw her face, I said,
" Earth has no fruits so fairly red
As these that swing above my head;
No purpled leaf, no poppied land,
Like this that lies in reach of hand."

And, soft, unto myself I said:
" O soul, inured to rue and rime,
To barren toil and bitter bread,
To biting rime, to bitter rue,
Earth is not Nazareth; be good.
O sacred Indian-summer time
Of scarlet fruits, of fragrant wood,
Of purpled clouds, of curling haze—
O days of golden dreams and days
Of banish'd, vanish'd tawny men,
Of martial songs and manly deeds—
Be fair to-day, and bear me true."
We mounted, turn'd the sudden steeds
Toward the yellow hills, and flew.

My faith! but she rode fair, and she
Had scarlet berries in her hair,
And on her hands white starry stones.
The satellites of many thrones
Fall down before her gracious air
In that full season.   Fair to see
Are pearly shells, red virgin gold,
And yellow fruits, and sun-down seas,
And babes sun-brown; but all of these,
And all fair things of sea besides,
Before the matchless, manifold
Accomplishments of her who rides
With autumn summer in her hair,
And knows her steed and holds her fair
And stately in her stormy seat,
They lie like playthings at her feet.

By heaven! she was more than fair,
And more than good, and matchless wise,
With all the lovelight in her eyes,
And all the midnight in her hair.

Through leafy avenues and lanes,
And lo! we climb'd the yellow hills,
With russet leaves about the brows

That reach'd from over-reaching trees.
With purpled briers to the knees
Of steeds that fretted foamy thews,
We turn'd to look a time below
Beneath the ancient arch of boughs,
That bent above us as a bow
Of promise, bound in many hues.

I reach'd my hand. I could refuse
All fruits but this, the touch of her
At such a time. But lo! she lean'd
With lifted face and soul, and leant
As leans devoutest worshipper,
Beyond the branches scarlet screen'd
And look'd above me and beyond,
So fix'd and silent, still and fond,
She seem'd the while she look'd to lose
Her very soul in such intent.
She look'd on other things, but I
I saw nor scarlet leaf nor sky;
I look'd on her, and only her.

Afar the city lay in smokes
Of battle, and the martial strokes
Of Progress thunder'd through the land

And struck against the yellow trees,
And roll'd in hollow echoes on
Like sounding limits of the seas
That smite the shelly shores at dawn.

Beyond, below, on either hand
There reach'd a lake in belt of pine,
A very dream; a distant dawn
Asleep in all the autumn shine,
Some like one of another land
That I once laid a hand upon,
And loved too well, and named as mine.

She sometimes touch'd with dimpled hand
The drifting mane with dreamy air,
She sometimes push'd aback her hair;
But still she lean'd and look'd afar,
As silent as the statues stand,—
For what? For falling leaf? For star,
That runs before the bride of death? . . .
The elements were still; a breath ·
Stirr'd not, the level western sun
Pour'd in his arrows every one;
Spill'd all his wealth of purpled red
On velvet poplar leaf below,

On arching chestnut overhead '
In all the hues of heaven's bow.

She sat the upper hill, and high.
I spurr'd my black steed to her side;
" The bow of promise, lo! " I cried,
And lifted up my eyes to hers
With all the fervid love that stirs
The blood of men beneath the sun,
And reach'd my hand, as one undone,
In suppliance to hers above:
"The bow of promise! give me love!
I reach a hand, I rise or fall,
Henceforth from this: put forth a hand
From your high place and let me stand—
Stand soul and body, white and tall!
Why, I would live for you, would die
To-morrow, but to live to-day,
Give me but love, and let me live
To die before you. I can pray
To only you, because I know,
If you but give what I bestow,
That God has nothing left to give."

Christ! still her stately head was raised,
And still she silent sat and gazed

Beyond the trees, beyond the town,
To where the dimpled waters slept,
Nor splendid eyes once bended down
To eyes that lifted up and wept.

She spake not, nor subdued her head
To note a hand or heed a word;
And then I question'd if she heard
My life-tale on that leafy hill,
Or any fervid word I said,
And spoke with bold, vehement will.

She moves, and from her bridled hand
She slowly drew the dainty glove,
Then gazed again upon the land.
The dimpled hand, a snowy dove
Alit, and moved along the mane
Of glossy skeins; then, overbold,
It fell across the mane, and lay
Before my eyes a sweet bouquet
Of cluster'd kisses, white as snow.
I should have seized it reaching so,
But something bade me back,—a ban;
Around the third fair finger ran
A shining, hateful hoop of gold.

Ay, then I turn'd, I look'd away,
I sudden felt forlorn and chill;
I whistled, like, for want to say,
And then I said, with bended head,
"Another's ship from other shores,
With richer freight, with fairer stores,
Shall come to her some day instead;"
Then turn'd about,— and all was still.

Yea, you had chafed at this, and cried,
And laugh'd with bloodless lips, and said
Some bitter things to sate your pride,
And toss'd aloft a lordly head,
And acted well some wilful lie,
And, most like, cursed yourself—but I . ..
Well, you be crucified, and you
Be broken up with lances through
The soul, then you may turn to find
Some ladder-rounds in keenest rods,
Some solace in the bitter rind,
Some favor with the gods irate—
The everlasting anger'd gods—
And ask not overmuch of fate.

I was not born, was never bless'd,
With cunning ways, nor wit, nor skill

In woman's ways, nor words of love,
Nor fashion'd suppliance of will.
A very clown, I think, had guess'd
How out of place and plain I seem'd;
I, I, the idol-worshipper,
Who saw nor maple-leaves nor sky
But took some touch and hue of her.

I am a pagan, heathen, lo!
A savage man, of savage lands;
Too quick to love, too slow to know
The sign that tame love understands.

* * * * *

Some heedless hoofs went sounding down
The broken way. The woods were brown,
And homely now; some idle talk
Of folk and town; a broken walk;
But sounding feet made song no more
For me along that leafy shore.

The sun caught up his gather'd sheaves;
A squirrel caught a nut, and ran;
A rabbit rustled in the leaves,
A whirling bat, black-wing'd and tan,
Blew swift between us; sullen night

Fell down upon us; mottled kine,
With lifted heads, went lowing down
The rocky ridge toward the town,
And all the woods grew dark as wine.

    *   *   *   *   *

Yea, bless'd Ohio's banks are fair;
A sunny clime and good to touch,
For tamer men of gentler mien,
But as for me, another scene.
A land below the Alps I know,
Set well with grapes and girt with much
Of woodland beauty; I shall share
My rides by night below the light
Of Mauna Loa, ride below
The steep and starry Hebron height;
Shall lift my hands in many lands,
See South Sea palm, see Northland fir,
See white-winged swans, see red-bill'd
    doves;
See many lands and many loves,
But never more the face of her.

And what her name or now the place
Of her who makes my Mecca's prayer,
Concerns you not; not any trace

Of entrance to my temple's shrine
Remains.   The memory is mine,
And none shall pass the portals there.

The present! take it, hold it thine,
But that one hour out from all
The years that are, or yet shall fall,
I pluck it out, I name it mine;
That hour bound in sunny sheaves,
With tassell'd shocks of golden shine,
That hour, wound in scarlet leaves,
Is mine. I stretch a hand and swear
An oath that breaks into a prayer;
By heaven, it is wholly mine!

I see the gold and purple gleam
Of autumn leaves, a reach of seas,
A silent rider like a dream
Moves by, a mist of mysteries,
And these are mine, and only these,
Yet they be more in my esteem,
Than silver'd sails on corall'd seas.

Let red-leaf'd boughs sweet fruits bestow,
Let fame of foreign lands be mine.

Let blame of faithless men befall;
It matters nothing; over all,
One hour arches like a bow
Of promise blent in many hues,
That tide nor time shall bid decline;
Or storms of all the years refuse.

BURNS.

ELD Druid oaks of Ayr.
        Precepts! Poems! Pages
Lessons! Leaves, and Volumes!
Arches! Pillars! Columns
In corridors of ages!
Grand patriarchal sages
Lifting palms in prayer!

The Druid beards are drifting
And shifting to and fro,
In gentle breezes lifting,
That bat-like come and go.
The while the moon is sifting
A sheen of shining snow
On all these blossoms lifting
Their blue eyes from below.

No, 'tis not phantoms walking
That you hear rustling there,
But bearded Druids talking,
And turning leaves in prayer.
No, not a night-bird singing
Nor breeze the broad bough swinging,
But that bough holds a censer,
And swings it to and fro.
'Tis Sunday eve, remember,
That's why they chant so low.

I LINGER in the autumn noon,
   I listen to the partridge call,
I watch the yellow leaflets fall
And drift adown the dimpled Doon.
I lean me o'er the ivy-grown
Auld brig, where Vandal tourists' tools
Have ribb'd out names that would be known,
Are known—known as a herd of fools.

Down Ailsa Craig the sun declines,
   With lances level'd here and there—
The tinted thorns! the trailing vines!
   O braes of Doon! so fond, so fair!
So passing fair, so more than fond!
The Poet's place of birth beyond,
   Beyond the mellow bells of Ayr!

I hear the milk-maid's twilight song
Come bravely through the storm-bent oaks;
Beyond, the white surf's sullen strokes
   Beat in a chorus deep and strong;
I hear the sounding forge afar,
And rush and rumble of the car,

The steady tinkle of the bell
Of lazy, laden, home-bound cows
That stop to bellow and to browse;
  I breathe the soft sea-wind as well.

  O Burns! where bide? where bide ye now?
Where are you in this night's full noon,
Great master of the pen and plough?
Might you not on yon slanting beam
Of moonlight, kneeling to the Doon,
Descend once to this hallow'd stream?
Sure yon stars yield enough of light
For heaven to spare your face one night.

  O Burns! another name for song,
Another name for passion—pride;
For love and poesy allied;
For strangely blended right and wrong.

  I picture you as one who kneel'd
A stranger at his own hearthstone;
One knowing all, yet all unknown,
One seeing all, yet all conceal'd;
The fitful years you linger'd here,
A lease of peril and of pain;

And I am thankful yet again
The gods did love you, ploughman! peer!

In all your own and other land,
I hear your touching songs of cheer;
The peasant and the lordly peer
Above your honor'd dust strike hands.

A touch of tenderness is shown
In this unselfish love of Ayr,
And it is well, you earn'd it fair;
For all unhelmeted, alone,
You proved a ploughman's honest claim
To battle in the lists of fame;
You earn'd it as a warrior earns
His laurels fighting for his land,
And died—it was your right to go.
O eloquence of silent woe!
The Master leaning reach'd a hand,
And whisper'd, "It is finish'd, Burns!"

O sad, sweet singer of a Spring!
Yours was a chill, uncheerful May,
And you knew no full days of June;
You ran too swiftly up the way,

And wearied soon, so over-soon!
You sang in weariness and woe;
You falter'd, and God heard you sing,
Then touch'd your hand and led you so,
You found life's hill-top low, so low,
You cross'd its summit long ere noon.
Thus sooner than one would suppose
Some weary feet do find repose.

BYRON.

*I*N men whom **men condemn as ill**
  I find so much of goodness still,
In men whom men pronounce divine
I find so much of sin and blot,
I hesitate to draw a line
Between *the two, where God has not.*

O COLD and cruel Nottingham!
   In disappointment and in tears,
Sad, lost, and lonely, here I am
To question, " Is this Nottingham,
Of which I dream'd for years and years?"
I seek in vain for name or sign
Of him who made this mould a shrine
A Mecca to the fair and fond
Beyond the seas, and still beyond.

Where white clouds crush their drooping
      wings
Against the snow-crown'd battlements,

And peaks that flash like silver tents;
Where Sacramento's fountain springs,
And proud Columbia frets his shore
Of sombre, boundless wood and wold,
And lifts his yellow sands of gold
In plaintive murmurs evermore;
Where snowy dimpled Tahoe smiles,
And where white breakers from the sea,
In solid phalanx knee to knee,
Surround the calm Pacific Isles,
Then run and reach unto the land
And spread their thin palms on the sand,—
Is he supreme—there understood:
The free can understand the free;
The brave and good the brave and good.

Yea, he did sin; who hath reveal'd
That he was more than man, or less?
Yet sinn'd no more, but less conceal'd
Than they who cloak'd their follies o'er,
And then cast stones in his distress.
He scorn'd to make the good seem more,
Or make the bitter sin seem less.
And so his very manliness
The seeds of persecution bore.

When all his fervid, wayward love
Brought back no olive-branch or dove,
Or love or trust from any one,
Proud, all unpitied and alone
He lived to make himself unknown,
Disdaining love and yielding none.
Like some high-lifted sea-girt stone
That could not stoop, but all the days,
With proud brow turning to the breeze,
Felt seas blown from the south, and seas
Blown from the north, and many ways,
He stood—a solitary light
In stormy seas and settled night—
Then fell, but stirr'd the seas as far
As winds and waves and waters are.

The meek-eyed stars are cold and white
And steady, fix'd for all the years;
The comet burns the wings of night,
And dazzles elements and spheres,
Then dies in beauty and a blaze
Of light, blown far through other days.

The poet's passion, sense of pride,
His lawless love, the wooing throng

Of sweet temptations that betide
The wild and wayward child of song,
The world knows not: I lift a hand
To ye who know, who understand.

*　　*　　*　　*　　*

The ancient Abbey's breast is broad,
And stout her massive walls of stone;
But let him lie, repose alone
Ungather'd with the great of God,
In dust, by his fierce fellow-man.
Some one, some day, loud-voiced will speak
And say the broad breast was not broad,
The walls of stone were all too weak
To hold the proud dust, in their plan;
The hollow of God's great right hand
Receives it; let it rest with God.

In sad but beautiful decay
Grey Hucknall kneels into the dust,
And, cherishing her sacred trust,
Does blend her clay with lordly clay.

No sign or cryptic stone or cross
Unto the passing world has said,
"He died, and we deplore his loss."

No sound of sandall'd pilgrims' tread
Disturbs the pilgrim's peaceful rest,
Or frets the proud, impatient breast.
The bat flits through the broken pane,
The black swift swallow gathers moss,
And builds in peace above his head,
Then goes, then comes, and builds again.

And it is well; not otherwise
Would he, the grand sad singer, will.
The serene peace of paradise
He sought—'tis his—the storm is still.
Secure in his eternal fame,
And blended pity and respect,
He does not feel the cold neglect,
And England does not fear the shame.

MYRRH.

L IFE knows no deed so beautiful
  As is the white cold coffin'd past;
This I may love nor be betray'd:
The dead are faithful to the last.
I am not spouseless—I have wed
A memory—a life that's dead.

FAREWELL! for here the ways at last
  Divide—diverge, like delta'd Nile.
Which after desert dangers pass'd
Of many and many a thousand mile,
As constant as a column stone,
Seeks out the sea, divorced—alone.

  And you and I have buried Love,
A red seal on the coffin's lid;
The clerk below, the Court above,
Pronounce it dead: the corpse is hid
And I who never cross'd your will
Consent...that you may have it still.

Farewell! a sad word easy said
And easy sung, I think, by some....
....I clutch'd my hands, I turn'd my head
In my endeavor and was dumb;
And when I should have said, Farewell,
I only murmur'd, " This is hell."

What recks it now whose was the blame?
But call it mine; for better used
Am I to wrong and cold disdain,
Can better bear to be accused
Of all that wears the shape of shame,
Than have you bear one touch of blame.

I set my face for power and place,
My soul is toned to sullenness,
My heart holds not one sign nor trace
Of love, or trust, or tenderness.
But you—your years of happiness
God knows I would not make them less.

And you will come some summer eve,
When wheels the white moon on her track,
And hear the plaintive night-bird grieve,
And see the crickets clad in black;

Alone—not far—a little spell,
And say, "Well, yes, he loved me well;"

And sigh, "Well, yes, I mind me now,
None were so bravely true as he;
And yet his love was tame somehow,
It was so truly true to me;
I wish'd his patient love had less
Of worship and of tenderness:

"I wish it still, for thus alone
There comes a keen reproach or pain,
A feeling I dislike to own;
Half yearnings for his voice again,
Half longings for his earnest gaze,
To know him mine always—always."

*   *   *   *   *

I make no murmur; steady, calm,
Sphinx-like I gaze on days ahead.
No wooing word, no pressing palm,
No sealing love with lips seal-red,
No waiting for some dusk or dawn,
No sacred hour....all are gone.

I go alone; no little hands

To lead me from forbidden ways,
No little voice in other lands
To cheer through all the weary days;
Yet these are yours, and that to me
Is much indeed....So let it be....

... A last look from my mountain wall ...
I watch the red sun wed the sea
Beside your home ... the tides will fall
And rise, but nevermore shall we
Stand hand in hand and watch them flow,
As we once stood ... Christ! this is so!

But, when the stately sea comes in
With measured tread and mouth afoam,
My darling cries above the din,
And asks, " Has father yet come home?"
Then look into the peaceful sky,
And answer, gently, " By and by."

    *   *   *   *   *

One deep spring in a desert sand,
One moss'd and mystic pyramid,
A lonely palm on either hand,
A fountain in a forest hid,

Are all my life has realized
Of all I cherish'd, all I prized:

Of all I dream'd in early youth
Of love by streams and love-lit ways,
While my heart held its type of truth
Through all the tropic golden days,
And I the oak, and you the vine,
Clung palm in palm through cloud or shine.

Some time when clouds hang overhead,
(What weary skies without one cloud!)
You may muse on this love that's dead,
Muse calm when not so cold or proud,
And say, " At last it comes to me,
That none was ever true as he."

My sin was that I loved too much—
But I enlisted for the war,
Till we the deep-sea shore should touch,
Beyond Atlanta—near or far—
And truer soldier never yet
Bore shining sword or bayonet.

I did not blame you—do not blame.
The stormy elements of soul

That I did scorn to tone or tame,
Or bind down unto dull control
In full fierce youth, they all are yours,
With all their folly and their force.

God keep you pure, oh, very pure,
God give you grace to dare and do;
God give you courage to endure
The all He may demand of you,—
Keep time-frosts from your raven hair,
And your young heart without a care.

I make no murmur nor complain;
Above me are the stars and blue
Alluring far to grand refrain;
Before, the beautiful and true,
To love or hate, to win or lose;
Lo! I will now arise, and choose.

But should you sometime read a sign,
A name among the princely few,
In isles of song beyond the brine,
Then you will think a time, and you
Will turn and say, " He once was mine,
Was all my own; his smiles, his tears
Were mine—were mine for years and years."

EVEN SO.

SIERRAS, and eternal tents
Of snow that flash o'er battlements
Of mountains! My land of the sun,
Am I not true? have I not done
All things for thine, for thee alone,
O sun-land, sea-land, thou mine own?
Be my reward some little place
To pitch my tent, some tree and vine
Where I may sit with lifted face,
And drink the sun as drinking wine:
Where sweeps the Oregon, and where
White storms are in the feather'd fir.

IN the shadows a-west of the sunset mountains,
  Where old-time giants had dwelt and peopled,
And built up cities and castled battlements,
And rear'd up pillars that pierced the heavens,
A poet dwelt, of the book of Nature—
An ardent lover of the pure and beautiful,
Devoutest lover of the true and beautiful.
Profoundest lover of the grand and beautiful—
With a heart all impulse, intensest passion,
Who believed in love as in God Eternal—
A dream while the waken'd world went over,
An Indian summer of the sullen seasons;

And he sang wild songs like the wind in cedars,
Was tempest-toss'd as the pines, yet ever
As fix'd in truth as they in the mountains.

He had heard a name as one hears of a
    princess,
Her glory had come unto him in stories;
From afar he had look'd as entranced upon her;
He gave her name to the wind in measures,
And he heard her name in the deep-voiced
    cedars,
And afar in the winds rolling on like the billows,
Her name in the name of another for ever
Gave all his numbers their grandest strophes;
He enshrined her image in his heart's high
    temple,
And saint-like held her, too sacred for mortal.

      *   *   *   *   *

He came to fall like a king of the forest
Caught in the strong stormy arms of the
    wrestler;
Forgetting his songs, his crags and his mount-
    ains,
And nearly his God, in his wild deep passion;

And when he had won her and turn'd him home-
      ward,
With the holiest pledges love gives its lover,

The mountain route was as strewn with roses.
Can a high love then be a thing unholy,
To make us better and bless'd supremely?
The day was fix'd for the feast and nuptials;
He crazed with impatience at the tardy hours;
He flew in the face of old Time as a tyrant;
He had fought the days that stood still between
      them,
One by one, as you fight with a foeman,
Had they been animate and sensate beings.

At last then the hour came coldly forward.
When Mars was trailing his lance on the mount-
      ains
He rein'd his steed and look'd down in the cañon
To where she dwelt, with a heart of fire;
He kiss'd his hand to the smoke slow curling,
Then bow'd his head in devoutest blessing.
His spotted courser did plunge and fret him
Beneath his gay and silk-fringed carona.
And toss his neck in a black mane banner'd;

Then all afoam, plunging iron-footed,
Dash'd him swift down with a wild impatience.

A coldness met him, like the breath of a
    cavern,
As he joyously hasten'd across the threshold.
She came, and coldly she spoke and scornful,
In answer to warm and impulsive passion.
All things did array them in shapes most hate-
    ful,
And life did seem but a jest intolerable.
He dared to question her why this estrange-
    ment:
She spoke with a strange and stiff indifference,
And bade him go on all alone life's journey.

Then stern and tall he did stand up before her,
And gaze dark-brow'd through the low narrow
    casement.
For a time, as if warring in thought with a pas-
    sion;
Then, crushing hard down the hot welling bit-
    terness,
He folded his form in a sullen silentness
And turn'd for ever away from her presence:

Bearing his sorrow like some great burden,
Like a black night-mare in his hot heart muffled;
With his faith in the truth of woman broken.

*   *   *   *   *

'Mid Theban pillars, where sang the Pindar,
Breathing the breath of the Grecian islands,
Breathing in spices and olive and myrtle,
Counting the caravans, curl'd and snowy,
Slow journeying over his head to Mecca
Or the high Christ-land of most holy memory,
Counting the clouds through the boughs above
    him,
That brush'd white marbles that time had
    chisel'd
And rear'd as tombs on the great dead city,
Letter'd with solemn but unread moral—
A poet rested in the red-hot summer.
He took no note of the things about him,
But dream'd and counted the clouds above him;
His soul was troubled, and his sad heart's Mecca
Was a miner's home far over the ocean,
Banner'd by pines that did brush blue heaven.

When the sun went down on the bronzed
    Morea,

He read to himself from the lines of sorrow
That came as a wail from the one he worshipp'd,
Sent over the seas by an old companion:
They spoke no word of him, or remembrance.
And he was most sad, for he felt forgotten,
And said: "In the leaves of her fair heart's
    album
She has cover'd my face with the face of another.
Let the great sea lift like a wall between us,
High-back'd, with his mane of white storms for
    ever—
I shall learn to love, I shall wed my sorrow,
I shall take as a spouse the days that are per-
    ish'd;
I shall dwell in a land where the march of
    genius
Made tracks in marble in the days of giants;
I shall sit in the ruins where sat the Marius,
Grey with the ghosts of the great departed."
And then he said in the solemn twilight . . .

"Strangely wooing are yon worlds above us,
Strangely beautiful is the Faith of Islam,
Strangely sweet are the songs of Solomon,
Strangely tender are the teachings of Jesus,

Strangely cold is the sun on the mountains,
Strangely mellow is the moon on old ruins,
Strangely pleasant are the stolen waters,
Strangely lighted is the North night-region,
Strangely strong are the streams in the ocean,
Strangely true are the tales of the Orient,
But stranger than all are the ways of women."

His head on his hands and his hands on the
        marble,
Alone in the moonlight he slept in the ruins;
And a form was before him white-mantled in
        moonlight,
And bitter he said to the one he had worshipp'd—

"Your hands in mine, your face, your eyes
Look level into mine, and mine
Are not abashed in anywise
As eyes were in an elder syne.
Perhaps the pulse is colder now,
And blood comes tamer to the brow
Because of hot blood long ago....
Withdraw your hand?....Well, be it so,
And turn your bent head slow sidewise,
For recollections are as seas

That come and go in tides, and these
Are flood-tides filling to the eyes,

" How strange that you above the vale
And I below the mountain wall
Should walk and meet!..Why, you are pale!..
Strange meeting on the mountain fringe!..
....More strange we ever met at all!....
Tides come and go, we know their time;
The moon, we know her wane or prime:
But who knows how the heart may hinge?

" You stand before me here to-night,
But not beside me, not beside—
Are beautiful, but not a bride.
Some things I recollect aright,
Though full a dozen years are done
Since we two met one winter night—
Since I was crush'd as by a fall;
For I have watch'd and pray'd through all
The shining circles of the sun.

" I saw you where sad cedars wave;
I sought you in the dewy eve
When shining crickets trill and grieve:
17

You smiled, and I became a slave.
A slave! I worshipp'd you at night,
When all the blue field blossom'd red
With dewy roses overhead
In sweet and delicate delight.
I was devout. I knelt that night
To Him who doeth all things well.
I tried in vain to break the spell;
My prison'd soul refused to rise
And image saints in Paradise,
While one was here before my eyes.

"Some things are sooner marr'd than made.
A frost fell on a soul that night,
A soul was black that erst was white.
And you forget the place—the night!
Forget that aught was done or said—
Say this has pass'd a long decade—
Say not a single tear was shed—
Say you forget these little things!
Is not your recollection loth?
Well, little bees have bitter stings,
And I remember for us both.

"No, not a tear. Do men complain?
The outer wound will show a stain,

And we may shriek at idle pain;
But pierce the heart, and not a word,
Or wail, or sign, is seen or heard.

"I did not blame—I do not blame,
My wild heart turns to you the same,
Such as it is; but oh, its meed
Of faithfulness and trust and truth,
And gushing confidence of youth,
I caution, you, is small indeed.

"I follow'd you, I worshipp'd you
And I would follow, worship still;
But if I felt the blight and chill
Of frosts in my uncheerful spring,
And show it now in riper years
In answer to this love you bring—
In answer to this second love,
This wail of an unmated dove,
In cautious answer to your tears—
You, you know who taught me disdain.
But deem you I would deal you pain?
I joy to know your heart is light,
I journey glad to know it thus,
And could I dare to make it less?
Yours—you are day, but I am night.

"God knows I would descend to-day
Devoutly on my knees, and pray
Your way might be one path of peace
Through bending boughs and blossom'd trees,
And perfect bliss through roses fair;
But know you, back—one long decade—
How fervently, how fond I pray'd?—
What was the answer to that prayer?

"The tale is old, and often told
And lived by more than you suppose—
The fragrance of a summer rose
Press'd down beneath the stubborn lid,
When sun and song are hush'd and hid,
And summer days are grey and old.

"We parted so.   Amid the bays
And peaceful palms and song and shade
Your cheerful feet in pleasure stray'd
Through all the swift and shining days.

"You made my way another way,
You bade it should not be with thine—
A fierce and cheerless route was mine:
But we have met, at last, to-day.

"You talk of tears—of bitter tears—
And tell of tyranny and wrong,
And I re-live some stinging jeers,
Back, far back, in the leaden years.
A lane without a turn is long,
I muse, and whistle a reply—
Then bite my lips to crush a sigh.

"You sympathize that I am sad,
I sigh for you that you complain,
I shake my yellow hair in vain,
I laugh with lips, but am not glad.

   * * * * *

. . . " His was a hot love of the hours,
And love and lover both are flown;
Now you walk, like a ghost, alone.
He sipp'd your sunny lips, and he
Took all their honey: now the bee
Bends down the heads of other flowers
And other lips lift up to kiss . . .
. . . I am not cruel, yet I find
A savage solace for the mind
And sweet delight in saying this . . .
Now you are silent, white, and you
Lift up your hands as making sign,

And your rich lips lie thin and blue
And ashen . . . and you writhe, and you
Breathe quick and tremble . . . is it true
The soul takes wounds, sheds blood like wine?

*   *   *   *   *

. . . "You seem so most uncommon tall
Against the lonely ghostly moon,
That hurries homeward oversoon,
And hides behind you and the pines;
And your two hands hang cold and small,
And your two thin arms lie like vines,
Or winter moonbeams on a wall.
. . . What if you be a weary ghost,
And I but dream, and dream I wake?
Then wake me not, and my mistake

Is not so bad: let's make the most
Of all we get, asleep, awake—
And waste not one sweet thing at all.
God knows that, at the best, life brings
The soul's share so exceeding small
We weary for some better things,
And hunger even unto death.
Laugh loud, be glad with ready breath,
For after all are joy and grief

Not merely matters of belief?
And what is certain, after all,
But death, delightful, patient death?
The cool and perfect, peaceful sleep,
Without one tossing hand, or deep
Sad sigh and catching in of breath!

" Be satisfied.   The price of breath
Is paid in toil.   But knowledge is
Bought only with a weary care,
And wisdom means a world of pain....
Well, we have suffered, will again,
And we can work and wait and bear,
Strong in the certainty of bliss.
Death is delightful: after death
Breaks in the dawn of perfect day.
Let question he who will: the may
Throws fragrance far beyond the wall.
I pass no word with such: 'tis fit
To pity such: therefore I say
Be wise and make the best of it;
Content and strong against the fall.

" Death is delightful.   Death is dawn.
Fame is not much, love is not much,

Yet what else is there worth the touch
Of lifted hand with dagger drawn?
So surely life is little worth:
Therefore I say, Look up; therefore
I say, One little star has more
Bright gold than all the earth of earth.

"Yet we must labor, plant to reap—
Life knows no folding up of hands—
Must plough the soul, as ploughing lands,
In furrows fashion'd strong and deep.
Life has its lesson.   Let us learn
The hard, long lesson from the birth,
And be content; stand breast to breast,
And bear and battle till the rest.
Yet I look to yon stars, and say.
Thank Christ, ye are so far away
That when I win you I can turn
And look, and see no sign of earth.

*   *   *   *   *

ABOVE THE CLOUDS.

MID white Sierras, that slope to the sea,
    Lie turbulent lands. Go dwell in the
      skies,
And the thundering tongues of Yosemite
Shall persuade you to silence, and you shall be
      wise.

I but sing for the love of song and the few
    Who loved me first and shall love me last;
    And the storm shall pass as the storms have
      pass'd,
For never were clouds but the sun came through.

INA.

SAD song of the wind in the mountains
   And the sea-wave of grass on the plain,
That breaks in bloom-foam by the fountains,
And forests, that breaketh again
On the mountains, as breaketh a main.

Bold thoughts that were strong as the grizzlies,
But now weak in their prison of words;
Bright fancies that flash'd like the glaciers,
Now dimm'd like the lustre of birds,
And butterfles huddled as herds.

Sad symphony, wild, and unmeasured,
Weed warp, and woof woven in strouds
Strange truths that a stray soul has treasured,
Truths seen as through folding of shrouds,
Or as stars through the rolling of clouds.

A Hacienda near Tezcuco, Mexico. Young DON
CARLOS *alone, looking out on the moonlit mount-*
ain.

DON CARLOS.

POPOCATAPETL looms lone like an island,
  Above white-cloud waves that break up
    against him;
Around him white buttes in the moonlight are
    flashing
Like silver tents pitch'd in the fair fields of
    heaven
While standing in line, in their snows everlast-
    ing,
Flash peaks, as my eyes into heaven are lifted,
Like milestones that lead to the city eternal.

Ofttime when the sun and the sea lay to-
    gether,
Red-welded as one, in their red bed of lovers,
Embracing and blushing like loves newly wed-
    ded,

I have trod on the trailing crape fringes of twi-
    light,
And stood there and listen'd, and lean'd with
    lips parted,
Till lordly peaks wrapp'd them, as chill night
    blew over,
In great cloaks of sable, like proud sombre
    Spaniards,
And stalk'd from my presence down night's
    corridors.

When the red-curtain'd West has bent red as
    with weeping
Low over the couch where the prone day lay
    dying,
I have stood with brow lifted, confronting the
    mountains
That held their white faces of snow in the
    heavens,
And said, " It is theirs to array them so purely,
Because of their nearness to the temple eter-
    nal;"
And child-like have said, " They are fair rest-
    ing places

For the dear weary dead on their way up to
    heaven."

  But my soul is not with you to-night, mighty
    mountains:
It is held to the levels of earth by an angel
Far more than a star, earth fall'n or unfall'n,
Yet fierce in her follies and headstrong and
    stronger
Than streams of the sea running in with the bil-
    lows.

  Very well. Let him woo, let him thrust his
    white whiskers
And lips pale and purple with death, in be-
    tween us;
Let her wed, as she wills, for the gold of the
    grey-beard.
I will set my face for you, O mountains, my
    brothers,
For I yet have my honor, my conscience and
    freedom,
My fleet-footed mustang and pistols rich sil-
    ver'd;
I will turn as the earth turns her back on the
    sun,

But return to the light of her eyes never more,
While noons have a night and white seas have
     a shore.

INA, *approaching.*

INA.

'I have come, dear Don Carlos, to say you fare-
     well,
I shall wed with Don Castro at dawn of to-
     morrow,
And be all his own—firm, honest and faithful.
I have promised this thing; that I keep my
     promise
You who do know me care never to question.
I have master'd myself to say this thing to you;
Hear me: be strong, then, and say adieu bravely;
The world is his own who will brave its bleak
     hours.
Dare, then, to confront the cold days in their
     column;
As they march down upon you, stand, hew them
     to pieces,
One after another, as you would a fierce foeman,
Till not one abideth between two true bosoms."

[DON CARLOS, *with a laugh of scorn, flies from the verandah, mounts horse, and disappears.*]

INA (*looking out into the night, after a long silence*).

How doleful the night-hawk screams in the
    heavens,
How dismally gibbers the grey coyote!
Afar to the south now the turbulent thunder,
Mine equal, my brother, my soul's own com-
    panion,
Talks low in his sleep, like a giant deep-troubled;
Talks fierce in accord with my own stormy spirit.

SCENE II.

Sunset on a spur of Mount Hood. LAMONTE *contemplates the scene.*

LAMONTE.

A FLUSH'D and weary messenger a-west
Is standing at the half-closed door of day,
As he would say, Good-night; and now his
bright
Red cap he tips to me and turns his face.
Were it an unholy thing to say, An angel now
Beside the door stood with uplifted seal?
Behold the door seal'd with that blood-red seal
Now burning, spreading o'er the mighty West.
Never again shall that dead day arise
Therefrom, but must be born and come anew.

The tawny, solemn Night, child of the East,
Her mournful robe trails o'er the distant woods,
And comes this way with firm and stately step.
Afront, and very high, she wears a shield,
A plate of silver, and upon her brow
The radiant Venus burns, a pretty lamp.

Behold! how in her gorgeous flow of hair
Do gleam a million mellow yellow gems,
That spill their molten gold upon the dewy
 grass.
Now throned on boundless plains, and gazing
 down
So calmly on the red-seal'd tomb of day,
She rests her form against the Rocky Mount-
 ains,
And rules with silent power a peaceful world.

'Tis midnight now.   The bent and broken
 moon.
All batter'd, black, as from a thousand battles,
Hangs silent on the purple walls of heaven.
The angel warrior, guard of the gates eternal,
In battle-harness girt, sleeps on the field:
But when to-morrow comes, when wicked men
That fret the patient earth are all astir,
He will resume his shield, and, facing earth-
 ward,
The gates of heaven guard from sins of earth.

'Tis morn. Behold the kingly day now leaps
The eastern wall of earth with sword in hand.

18

And clad in flowing robe of mellow light,
Like to a king that has regain'd his throne,
He warms his drooping subjects into joy,
That rise renewed to do him fealty,
And rules with pomp the universal world.

Don Carlos *ascends the mountain gesticulating and talking to himself.*

Don Carlos.

Oh for a name that black-eyed maids would
    sigh
And lean with parted lips at mention of;
That I should seem so tall in minds of men
That I might walk beneath the arch of heaven,
And pluck the ripe red stars as I pass'd on,
As favor'd guests do pluck the purple grapes
That hang above the humble entrance-way
Of palm-thatch'd mountain-inn of Mexico,
Oh, I would give the green leaves of my life
For something grand, for real and undream'd
    deeds!
To wear a mantle, broad and richly gemm'd
As purple heaven fringed with gold at sunset;
To wear a crown as dazzling as the sun,

And, holding up a sceptre lightning-charged,
Stride out among the stars as I have strode
A barefoot boy among the buttercups.
Alas! I am so restless. There is that
Within me doth rebel and rise against
The all I am and half I see in others;
And were't not for contempt of coward act
Of flying all defeated from the world,
As if I fear'd and dared not face its ills,
I should ere this have known, known more or
    less
Than any flesh that frets this sullen earth.
I know not where such thoughts will lead me to:
I have had fear that they would drive me mad,
And then have flatter'd my weak self, and said
The soul's outgrown the body—yea, the soul
Aspires to the stars, and in its struggles
Does make the dull flesh quiver like an aspen.

LAMONTE.

What waif is this cast here upon my shore,
From seas of subtle and most selfish men?

DON CARLOS.

Of subtle and most selfish men!—ah, that's
    the term!

And if you be but earnest in your spleen,
And other sex across man's shoulders lost,
I'll stand beside you on this crag and howl
And hurl my clench'd fists down upon their
      heads,
Till I am hoarse as yonder cataract.

LAMONTE.

Why, no, my friend, I'll not consent to that.
No true man yet has ever woman cursed.
And I—I do not hate my fellow man.
For man by nature bears within himself
Nobility that makes him half a god;
But as in somewise he hath made himself,
His universal thirst for gold and pomp,
And purchased fleeting fame and bubble honors,
Forgetting good, so mocking helpless age,
And rushing rough-shod o'er lowly merit,
I hold him but a sorry worm indeed;
And so have turn'd me quietly aside
To know the majesty of peaceful woods.

DON CARLOS (*as if alone*).

The fabled fount of youth led many fools,
Zealous in its pursuit, to hapless death;

And yet this thirst for fame, this hot ambition,
This soft-toned syren-tongue, enchanting Fame,
Doth lead me headlong on to equal folly,
Like to a wild bird charm'd by shining coils
And swift mesmeric glance of deadly snake:
I would not break the charm, but win a world
Or die with curses blistering my lips.

LAMONTE.

Give up ambition, fame and pride—
By pride the angels fell.

DON CARLOS.

By pride they reached a place from whence to
    fall.

LAMONTE.

You startle me!   I am unused to hear
Men talk these fierce and bitter thoughts; and
    yet
In closed recesses of my soul was once
A dark and gloomy chamber where they dwelt.
Give up ambition—yea, crush such thoughts
As you would crush from hearth a scorpion
    brood:

For, mark me well, they'll get the mastery,
And drive you on to death—or worse, across
A thousand ruin'd homes and broken hearts.

Don Carlos.

Give up ambition!   Oh, rather than die
And glide a lonely, nameless, shivering ghost
Down some dark tide of utter nothingness,
I'd write a name in blood and orphans' tears.
The temple-burner wiser was than kings.

Lamonte.

And would you dare the curse of man and—

Don Carlos.
                              Dare!
I'd dare the fearful curse of God!
I'd build a pyramid of the whitest skulls,
And step therefrom unto the spotted moon,
And thence to stars, and thence to central suns.
Then with one grand and mighty leap would
        land
Unhinder'd on the shore of gods of old.
There, sword in hand, unbared and unabash'd,

Would stand bold forth in presence of the God
Of gods and on the jewell'd inner-side
The walls of heaven, carve with keen Damascus
Steel, and, highest up, a grand and titled name
That time nor tide could touch or tarnish ever.

LAMONTE.

Seek not to crop above the heads of men
To be a better mark for envy's shafts.
Come to my peaceful home, and leave behind
These stormy thoughts and daring aspirations.
An earthly power's a thing comparative.
Is not a petty chief of some lone isle,
With half-a-dozen nude and starving subjects,
As much a king as he the Czar of Rusk?
In yonder sweet retreat and balmy place
I'll abdicate, and you be chief indeed.
There you will reign and tell me of the world,
Its life and lights, its sins and sickly shadows.
The pheasant will reveille beat at morn,
And rouse us to the battle of the day.
My swarthy subjects will in circle sit,
And, gazing on your noble presence, deem
You great indeed, and call you chief of chiefs;
And, knowing no one greater than yourself

In all the leafy borders of your realm,
'Gainst what can pride or poor ambition chafe?

'Twill be a kingdom without king, save you,
More broad than that the cruel Cortes won,
With subjects truer than he ever knew,
That know no law but only Nature's law,
And no religion know but that of love.
There truth and beauty are, for there is Nature,
Serene and simple. She will be our priestess,
And in her calm and uncomplaining face
Why we will read well her rubric and be wise.

DON CARLOS.

Why, truly now, this fierce and broken land,
Seen through your eyes, assumes a fairer shape.
Lead up, for you are nearer God than I.

Scene III.

Ina, *in black, alone. Midnight.*

Ina.

I WEEP? I weep? I laugh to think of it!
  I lift my dark brow to the breath of the
    ocean,
Soft kissing me now like the lips of my mother,
And laugh low and long as I crush the brown
    grasses,
To think I should weep! Why, I never wept—
    never,
Not even in punishments dealt me in childhood!
Yea, all of my wrongs and my bitterness buried
In my brave baby heart, all alone and un-
    friended.
And I pitied, with proud and disdainfullest pity,
The weak who would weep, and I laugh'd at
    the folly
Of those who could laugh and make merry with
    playthings.

I will not weep now over that I desired.
Desired? Yes: I to myself dare confess it,

Ah, too, to the world should it question too
    closely,
And bathe me and sport in a deep sea of candor.
  Let the world be deceived: it insists upon it:
Let it bundle me round in its black woe-gar-
    ments;
But I, self with self—my free soul fearless—
Am frank as the sun, nor the toss of a copper
Care I if the world call it good or evil.
I am glad to-night, and in new-born freedom
Forget all earth with my old companions,—
The moon and the stars and the moon-clad
    ocean.
I am face to face with the stars that know me,
And gaze as I gazed in the eyes of my mother,
Forgetting the city and the coarse things in it;
For there's naught but God in the shape of
    mortal,
Save one—my wandering, wild boy-lover—
That I do esteem worth a stale banana.

  The air hangs heavy and is warm on my
    shoulder,
And is thick with odors of balm and of blossom;
The great bay sleeps with the ships on her bosom;

Through the Golden Gate, to the left-hand
    yonder,
The white sea lies in a deep sleep, breathing,
The father of melody, mother of measure.

SCENE IV.

*A Wood by a rivulet on a spur of Mount Hood,
overlooking the Columbia. LAMONTE and DON
CARLOS, on their way to the camp, are reposing
under the shadow of the forest. Some deer are
observed descending to the brook, and DON CAR-
LOS seizes his rifle.*

LAMONTE.

NAY, nay, my friend, strike not from your
      covert so,
Strike like a serpent in the grass well hidden?
What, steal into their homes, and, when athirst
And unsuspecting, they come down in couples
And dip brown muzzles in the mossy brink,
Then shoot them down without chance to fly—
The only means that God has given them,
Poor, unarm'd mutes, to baffle man's cunning?
Ah, now I see you had not thought of this!
The hare is fleet, and is most quick at sound,
His coat is changed with all the changing fields;
Yon deer turn brown whene'er the leaves turn
      brown;

The dog has teeth, the cat has teeth and claws
And man has craft and art and sinewy arms:
All things that live have some means of defence.
All, all—save only lovely woman.

Don Carlos.

Nay, woman has her tongue—arm'd to the
    teeth.

Lamonte.

Thou Timon, what can 'scape your bitterness?
But for this sweet content of Nature here,
Upon whose breast we now recline and rest,
Why, you might lift your voice and rail at her!

Don Carlos.

Oh, I am out of patience with your faith!
What! She content and peaceful, uncomplain-
    ing?
I've seen her fretted like a lion caged,
Chafe like a peevish woman cross'd and churl'd,
Tramping and foaming like a whelpless bear;
Have seen her weep till earth was wet with
    tears,
Then turn all smiles—a jade that won her point?

Have seen her tear the hoary hair of Ocean,
While he, himself full half a world, would moan
And roll and toss his clumsy hands all day
To earth like some great helpless babe, that lay
Rude-rock'd and cradled by an unseen nurse,
Then stain her snowy hem with salt-sea tears;
And when the peaceful, mellow moon came
        forth,
To walk and meditate among the blooms
That make so blest the upper purple fields,
This wroth dyspeptic sea ran after her
With all his soul, as if to pour himself,
All sick and helpless, in her snowy lap.

Content!   Oh, she has crack'd the ribs of
        earth
And made her shake poor trembling man from
        off
Her back, e'en as a grizzly shakes the hounds;
She has upheaved her rocky spine against
The flowing robes of the Eternal God.

LAMONTE.

There once was one of nature like to this:
He stood a barehead boy upon a cliff

Pine-crown'd, that hung high o'er a bleak north
    sea.
His long hair stream'd and flash'd like yellow
    silk,
His sea-blue eyes lay deep and still as lakes
O'erhung by mountains arch'd in virgin snow;
And far astray, and friendless and alone,
A tropic bird blown through the north frost-
    wind,
He stood above the sea in the cold white moon,
His thin face lifted to the flashing stars.
He talk'd familiarly and face to face
With the Eternal God, in solemn night,
Confronting Him with free and flippant air
As one confronts a merchant o'er his counter,
And in vehement blasphemy did say:
" God, put aside this world—show me another!
God, this world's a cheat—hand down another!
I will not buy—not have it as a gift.
Put this aside and hand me down another—
Another, and another, still another,
Till I have tried the fairest world that hangs
Upon the walls and broad dome of your shop.
For I am proud of soul and regal born,
And will not have a cheap and cheating world."

Don Carlos.

The noble youth! So God gave him another?

Lamonte.

A bear, as in old time, came from the woods
And tare him there upon that storm-swept cliff—
A grim and grizzled bear, like unto hunger.
A tall ship sail'd adown the sea next morn,
And, standing with his glass upon the prow,
The captain saw a vulture on a cliff,
Gorging, and pecking, stretching his long neck,
Bracing his raven plumes against the wind,
Fretting the tempest with his sable feathers.

A Young Poet *ascends the mountain and approaches.*

Don Carlos.

Ho! ho! whom have we here? Talk of the
    devil,
And he's at hand. Say, who are you, and whence?

Poet.

I am a poet, and dwell down by the sea.

Don Carlos.

A poet! a poet, forsooth! A hungry fool!

Would you know what it means to be a poet
      now?
It is to want a friend, to want a home,
A country, money,—ay, to want a meal.
It is not wise to be a poet now,
For, oh, the world it has so modest grown
It will not praise a poet to his face,
But waits till he is dead some hundred years,
Then uprears marbles cold and stupid as itself.

                        [POET *rises to go.*

DON CARLOS.

Why, what's the haste? You'll reach there
    soon enough.

POET.

Reach where?

DON CARLOS.

The Inn to which all earthly roads do tend:
The "neat apartments furnish'd—see within;"
The "furnish'd rooms for quiet, single gentle-
    men;"
The narrow six-by-two where you will lie
With cold blue nose up-pointing to the grass,

Labell'd and box'd, and ready all for shipment.

POET (*loosening hair and letting fall a mantle*).

  Ah me! My Don Carlos, look kindly upon
      me!
With my hand on your arm and my dark brow
      lifted
Full level to yours, do you not now know me?
'Tis your own, own INA, you loved by the ocean,
In the warm-spiced winds from the far Cathay.

       DON CARLOS (*bitterly*).

  With the smell of the dead man still upon you!
Your dark hair wet from his death-damp fore-
      head!
You are not my Ina, for she is a memory.
A marble chisell'd, in my heart's dark chamber
Set up for ever, and naught can change her;
And you are a stranger, and the gulf between us
Is wide as the Plains, and as deep as Pacific.

  And now, good-night. In your serape folded
Hard by in the light of the pine-knot fire,
Sleep you as sound as you will be welcome;
And on the morrow— now mark me, madam—

When to-morrow comes, why, you will turn you
To the right or left as did Father Abram.
Good-night, for ever and for aye, good-bye;
My bitter is sweet and your truth is a lie.

INA (*letting go his arm and stepping back*).

Well then! 'tis over, and 'tis well thus ended;
I am well escaped from my life's devotion.
The waters of bliss are a waste of bitterness;
The day of joy I did join hands over,
As a bow of promise when my years were weary,
And set high up as a brazen serpent
To look upon when I else had fainted
In burning deserts, while you sipp'd ices
And snowy sherbets and roam'd unfetter'd,
Is a deadly asp in the fruit and flowers
That you in your bitterness now bear to me;
But its fangs unfasten and it glides down from
    me,
From a Cleopatra of cold white marble.

I have but done what I would do over,
Did I find one worthy of so much devotion;
And, standing here with my clean hands folded
Above a bosom whose crime is courage,

The only regret that my heart discovers
Is that I should do and have dared so greatly
For the love of one who deserved so little.

   Nay! say no more, nor attempt to approach
       me!
This ten-feet line lying now between us
Shall never be less while the land has measure.
See! night is forgetting the east in the heavens;
The birds pipe shrill and the beasts howl
       answer.

JOAQUIN MURIETTA.

GLINTINGS of day in the darkness,
Flashings of flint and of steel,
Blended in gossamer texture
The ideal and the real,
Limn'd like the phantom-ship shadow,
Crowding up under the keel.

I STAND beside the mobile sea;
And sails are spread, and sails are furl'd
From farthest corners of the world
And fold like white wings wearily.
Some ships go up, and some go down
In haste, like traders in a town.

Afar at sea some white shapes flee,
With arms stretch'd like a ghost's to me,
And cloud-like sails are blown and curl'd,
Then glide down to the under-world.
As if blown bare in winter blasts
Of leaf and limb, tall naked masts
Are rising from the restless sea.
I seem to see them gleam and shine
With clinging drops of dripping brine.

Broad still brown wings flit here and there,
Thin sea-blue wings wheel everywhere,   .
And white wings whistle through the air;
I hear a thousand sea-gulls call.

  Behold the ocean on the beach
Kneel lowly down as if in prayer,
I hear a moan as of despair,
While far at sea do toss and reach
Some things so like white pleading hands.
The ocean's thin and hoary hair
Is trail'd along the silver'd sands,
At every sigh and sounding moan.
The very birds shriek in distress
And sound the ocean's monotone.
'Tis not a place for mirthfulness,
But meditation deep, and prayer,
And kneelings on the salted sod,
Where man must own his littleness
And know the mightiness of God.

  Dared I but say a prophecy,
As sang the holy men of old,
Of rock-built cities yet to be
Along these shining shores of gold,

Crowding athirst into the sea,
What wondrous marvels might be told!
Enough, to know that empire here
Shall burn her loftiest, brightest star;
Here art and eloquence shall reign,
As o'er the wolf-rear'd realm of old;
Here learn'd and famous from afar,
To pay their noble court, shall come,
And shall not seek or see in vain,
But look on all with wonder dumb.

Afar the bright Sierras lie
A swaying line of snowy white,
A fringe of heaven hung in sight
Against the blue base of the sky.

I look along each gaping gorge,
I hear a thousand sounding strokes
Like giants rending giant oaks,
Or brawny Vulcan at his forge;
I see pick-axes flash and shine
And great wheels whirling in a mine.
Here winds a thick and yellow thread,
A moss'd and silver stream instead;
And trout that leap'd its rippled tide
Have turn'd upon their sides and died.

Lo! when the last pick in the mine
Lies rusting red with idleness,
And rot yon cabins in the mold,
And wheels no more croak in distress,
And tall pines re-assert command
Sweet bards along this sunset shore
Their mellow melodies will pour;
Will charm as charmers very wise,
Will strike the harp with master hand·
Will sound unto the vaulted skies,
The valor of these men of old—
The mighty men of 'Forty-nine;
Will sweetly sing and proudly say,
Long, long agone there was a day
When there were giants in the land.

* * * * *

Now who rides rushing on the sight
Hard down yon rocky long defile,
Swift as an eagle in his flight,
Fierce as a winter's storm at night
Blown from the bleak Sierra's height?
Such reckless rider!—I do ween
No mortal man his like has seen.
And yet, but for his long serape
All flowing loose, and black as crape,

And long silk locks of blackest hair
All streaming wildly in the breeze,
You might believe him in a chair,
Or chatting at some country fair
He rides so grandly at his ease.

But now he grasps a tighter rein,
A red rein wrought in golden chain,
And in his tapidaros stands,
Half turns and shakes two bloody hands,
And shouts defiance at his foe.
And now he calmly bares his brow
As if to challenge fate, and now
His hand drops to his saddle-bow
And clutches something gleaming there
As is to something more than dare.

The stray winds lift the raven curls,
Soft as a fair Castilian girl's,
And press a brow so full and high
Its every feature does belie
The thought he is compell'd to fly;
A brow as open as the sky
On which you gaze and gaze again
As on a picture you have seen

And often sought to see in vain,
That seems to hold a tale of woe
Or wonder, that you fain would know;
A brow cut deep as with a knife,
With many a dubious deed in life;
A brow of blended pride and pain.
And yearnings for what should have been.

Again he grasps his gutt'ring rein,
And wheeling like a hurricane,
Defying wood, or stone, or flood,
Is dashing down the gorge again.
Oh, never yet has prouder steed
Borne master nobler in his need!
There is a glory in his eye
That seems to dare and to defy
Pursuit, or time, or space, or race.
His body is the type of speed,
While from his nostril to his heel
Are muscles as if made of steel.

What crimes have made that red hand red?
What wrongs have written that young face
With lines of thought so out of place?
Where flies he?   And from whence has fled?

And what his lineage and race?
What glitters in his heavy belt,
And from his furr'd catenas gleam?
What on his bosom that doth seem
A diamond bright or dagger's hilt?
The iron hoofs that still resound
Like thunder from the yielding ground
Alone reply; and now the plain,
Quick as you breathe and gaze again,
Is won, and all pursuit is vain.

  * * * * *

I stand upon a stony rim,
Stone-paved and pattern'd as a street;
A rock-lipp'd cañon plunging south,
As if it were earth's open'd mouth,
Yawns deep and darkling at my feet;
So deep, so distant, and so dim
Its waters wind, a yellow thread,
And call so faintly and so far,
I turn aside my swooning head.
I feel a fierce impulse to leap
Adown the beetling precipice,
Like some lone, lost, uncertain star;
To plunge into a place unknown,
And win a world all, all my own;

Or if I might not meet that bliss,
At least escape the curse of this.

I gaze again. A gleaming star
Shines back as from some mossy well
Reflected from blue fields afar.
Brown hawks are wheeling here and there,
And up and down the broken wall
Clings clumps of dark green chaparral,
While from the rent rocks, grey and bare,
Blue junipers hang in the air.

Here, cedars sweep the stream and here,
Among the boulders moss'd and brown
That time and storms have toppled down
From towers undefiled by man,
Low cabins nestle as in fear,
And look no taller than a span.
From low and shapeless chimneys rise
Some tall straight columns of blue smoke,
And weld them to the bluer skies;
While sounding down the sombre gorge
I hear the steady pick-axe stroke,
As if upon a flashing forge.

*   *   *   *   *

Another scene, another sound!—
Sharp shots are fretting through the air,
Red knives are flashing everywhere,
And here and there the yellow flood
Is purpled with warm smoking blood.
The brown hawk swoops low to the ground,
And nimble chip-munks, small and still,
Dart striped lines across the sill
That lordly feet shall press no more.
The flume lies warping in the sun,
The pan sits empty by the door,
The pick-axe on its bed-rock floor
Lies rusting in the silent mine.
There comes no single sound nor sign
Of life, beside yon monks in brown
That dart their dim shapes up and down
The rocks that swelter in the sun;
But dashing down yon rocky spur,
Where scarce a hawk would dare to whirr,
Fly horsemen reckless in their flight.
One wears a flowing black capote,
While down the cape doth flow and float
Long locks of hair as dark as night,
And hands are red that erst were white.

All up and down the land to-day
Black desolation and despair
It seems have sat and settled there,
With none to frighten them away.
Like sentries watching by the way
Black chimneys topple in the air,
And seem to say, Go back, beware!
While up around the mountain's rim
Are clouds of smoke, so still and grim
They look as they are fasten'd there.

A lonely stillness, so like death,
So touches, terrifies all things,
That even rooks that fly o'erhead
Are hush'd, and seem to hold their breath,
To fly with muffled wings,
And heavy as if made of lead.
Some skulls that crumble to the touch,
Some joints of thin and chalk-like bone,
A tall black chimney, all alone,
That leans as if upon a crutch,
Alone are left to mark or tell,
Instead of cross or cryptic stone,
Where fair maids loved or brave men fell.

*   *   *   *   *

The sun is red and flush'd and dry,
And fretted from his weary beat
Across the hot and desert sky,
And swollen as from overheat,
And failing too; for see, he sinks
Swift as a ball of burnish'd ore:
It may be fancy, but methinks
He never fell so fast before.

I hear the neighing of hot steeds,
I see the marshalling of men
That silent move among the trees
As busily as swarming bees
With step and stealthiness profound,
On carpetings of spindled weeds,
Without a syllable or sound
Save clashing of their burnish'd arms,
Clinking dull death-like alarms—
Grim bearded men and brawny men
That grope among the ghostly trees.
Were ever silent men as these?
Was ever sombre forest deep
And dark as this?   Here one might sleep
While all the weary years went round,
Nor wake nor weep for sun or sound.

A stone's-throw to the right, a rock
Has rear'd his head among the stars—
An island in the upper deep—
And on his front a thousand scars
Of thunder's crash and earthquake's shock
Are seam'd as if by sabre's sweep
Of gods, enraged that he should rear
His front amid their realms of air.

What moves along his beetling brow,
So small, so indistinct and far,
This side yon blazing evening star,
Seen through that redwood's shifting
        bough?
A look-out on the world below?
A watcher for the friend—or foe?
This still troop's sentry it must be,
Yet seems no taller than my knee.

But for the grandeur of this gloom,
And for the chafing steeds' alarms,
And brown men's sullen clash of arms,
This were but as a living tomb.
These weeds are spindled, pale and white,
As if nor sunshine, life, nor light

Had ever reach'd this forest's heart.
Above, the red-wood boughs entwine
As dense as copse of tangled vine—
Above, so fearfully afar,
It seems as 'twere a lesser sky,
A sky without a moon or star,
The moss'd boughs are so thick and high.
At every lisp of leaf I start!
Would I could hear a cricket trill,
Or that yon sentry from his hill
Might shout or show some sign of life,
The place does seem so deathly still.
"Mount ye, and forward for the strife!"
Who by yon dark trunk sullen stands,
With black serape and bloody hands,
And coldly gives his brief command?

They mount—away! Quick on his heel
He turns and grasps his gleaming steel—
Then sadly smiles, and stoops to kiss
An upturn'd face so sweetly fair,
So sadly, saintly, purely fair
So rich of blessedness and bliss!
I know she is not flesh and blood,
But some sweet spirit of this wood;

20

I know it by her wealth of hair,
And step on the unyielding air;
Her seamless robe of shining white,
Her soul-deep eyes of darkest night;
But over all and more than all
That can be said or can befall,
That tongue can tell or pen can trace,
That wondrous witchery of face.

Between the trees I see him stride
To where a red steed fretting stands
Impatient for his lord's commands:
And she glides noiseless at his side.

One hand toys with her waving hair,
Soft lifting from her shoulders bare;
The other holds the loosen'd rein,
And rests upon the swelling mane
That curls the curved neck o'er and o'er,
Like waves that swirl along the shore.
He hears the last retreating sound
Of iron on volcanic stone,
That echoes far from peak to plain,
And 'neath the dense wood's sable zone,
He peers the dark Sierras down.

His hand forsakes her raven hair,
His eyes have an unearthly glare;
She shrinks and shudders at his side,
Then lifts to his her moisten'd eyes,
And only looks her sad replies.
A sullenness his soul enthrals,
A silence born of hate and pride;
His fierce volcanic heart so deep
Is stirr'd, his teeth, despite his will,
Do chatter as if in a chill;
His very dagger at his side

Does shake and rattle in its sheath,
As blades of brown grass in a gale
Do rustle on the frosted heath:
And yet he does not bend or weep.

As gently as a mother bows
Her first-born sleeping babe above,
The cherish'd cherub lips to kiss
In her full blessedness and bliss,
He bends to her with stately air,
His proud head in its cloud of hair.
I do not hear the hallow'd kiss;
I do not hear the hurried vows

Of passion, faith, unfailing love;
I do not mark the prison'd sighs,
I do not meet the moisten'd eyes.

A low sweet melody is heard
Like cooing of some Balize bird,
So fine it does not touch the air,
So faint it stirs not anywhere;
Faint as the falling of the dew,
Low as a pure unutter'd prayer,
The meeting, mingling, as it were,
In that one long, last, silent kiss
Of souls in paradisal bliss.

Erect, again he grasps the rein
So tight, as to the seat he springs,
I see his black steed plunge and poise
And beat the air with iron feet,
And curve his noble glossy neck,
And toss on high his swelling mane,
And leap—away! he spurns the rein!
He flies so fearfully and fleet,
But for the hot hoofs' ringing noise
'Twould seem as if he were on wings.

And she is gone! Gone like a breath,
Gone like a white sail seen at night

A moment, and then lost to sight;
Gone like a star you look upon,
That glimmers to a bead, a speck,
Then softly melts into the dawn,
And all is still and dark as death.

NOTE.—After the cruel conquest of California from Mexico, we poured in upon the simple and hospitable people from all parts of the United States. Strangers in language and religion, let it be honestly admitted, we were often guilty of gross wrong to the conquered Californians. Out of this wrong suddenly sprang Joaquin Murietta, a mere boy, and yet one of the boldest men in history. He led his men to the mountains and defied the army. But he soon degenerated into a robber, and a large reward was offered for his head. He was not yet twenty-two when killed. His head, I believe, is still on exhibition in San Francisco. I tell this with shame and horror. The splendid daring and unhappy death of this remarkable youth appeal strongly to me; and, bandit as he was, I am bound to say I have a great respect for his memory.

THE END.

The Poetical and Prose Works of
ELLA WHEELER WILCOX

Mrs. Wilcox's writings have been the inspiration of many young men and women. Her hopeful, practical, masterful views of life give the reader new courage in the very reading and are a wholesome spur to flagging effort. Words of truth so vital that they live in the reader's memory and cause him to think—to his own betterment and the lasting improvement of his own work in the world, in whatever line it lies—flow from this talented woman's pen.

MAURINE

Is a love story told in exquisite verse. "An ideal poem about as true and lovable a woman as ever poet created." It has repeatedly been compared with Owen Meredith's *Lucile.* In point of human interest it excels that noted story.

"Maurine" is issued in an *edition de luxe,* where the more important incidents of the story are portrayed by means of photographic studies from life.

Presentation Edition, 12mo, olive green cloth............$1.00
De Luxe Edition, white vellum, gold top.................... 1.50
New Illustrated Edition, extra cloth, gold top............. 1.50
De Luxe New Illustrated Edition, white vellum, gold top, 2.00

POEMS OF POWER.

New and revised edition. This beautiful volume contains more than *one hundred new poems,* displaying this popular poet's well-known taste, cultivation, and originality. The author says: "The final word in the title of the volume refers to the Divine power in every human being, the recognition of which is the secret of all success and happiness. It is this idea which many of the verses endeavor to inculcate and to illustrate."

"The lines of Mrs. Wilcox show both sweetness and strength."—*Chicago American.* "Ella Wheeler Wilcox has a strong grip upon the affections of thousands all over the world. Her productions are read to-day just as eagerly as they were when her fame was new, no other divinity having yet risen to take her place."—*Chicago Record-Herald.*

Presentation Edition, 12mo, dark blue cloth..............$1.00
De Luxe Edition, white vellum, gold top.................... 1.50

THREE WOMEN. A STORY IN VERSE.

"THREE WOMEN is the best thing I have ever done."—*Ella Wheeler Wilcox.*

This marvelous dramatic poem will compel instant praise because it touches every note in the scale of human emotion. It is intensely interesting, and will be read with sincere relish and admiration.

Presentation Edition, 12mo, light red cloth..............$1.00
De Luxe Edition, white vellum, gold top... .... 1.50

AN ERRING WOMAN'S LOVE.

There is always a fascination in Mrs. Wilcox's verse, but in these beautiful examples of her genius she shows a wonderful knowledge of the human heart.

"Ella Wheeler Wilcox has impressed many thousands of people with the extreme beauty of her philosophy and the exceeding usefulness of her point of view."—*Boston Globe*.

"Mrs. Wilcox stands at the head of feminine writers, and her verses and essays are more widely copied and read than those of any other American literary woman."—*New York World*. "Power and pathos characterize this magnificent poem. A deep understanding of life and an intense sympathy are beautifully expressed."—*Chicago Tribune*.

Presentation Edition, 12mo, light brown cloth...........$1.00
De Luxe Edition, white vellum, gold top................... 1.50

MEN, WOMEN AND EMOTIONS.

A skilful analysis of social habits, customs and follies. A common-sense view of life from its varied standpoints. . . . full of sage advice.

"These essays tend to meet difficulties that arise in almost every life. . . . Full of sound and helpful admonition, and is sure to assist in smoothing the rough ways of life wherever it be read and heeded."—*Pittsburg Times*.

12mo, heavy enameled paper...............................$0.50
Presentation Edition, dark brown cloth................... 1.00

THE BEAUTIFUL LAND OF NOD.

A collection of poems, songs, stories, and allegories dealing with child life. The work is profusely illustrated with dainty line engravings and photographs from life.

"The delight of the nursery; the foremost baby's book in the world."—*N. O. Picayune*.

Quarto, sage green cloth.................................$1.00

W. B. CONKEY COMPANY, - **Hammond, Indiana**

www.ingramcontent.com/pod-product-compliance
Lightning Source LLC
Chambersburg PA
CBHW060550030726
47498CB00005B/1332